A CHRISTMAS HAVEN

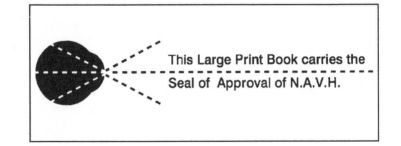

This Large Print Book carries the
Seal of Approval of N.A.V.H.

A CHRISTMAS HAVEN

AN AMISH CHRISTMAS ROMANCE

CINDY WOODSMALL
& ERIN WOODSMALL

THORNDIKE PRESS
A part of Gale, a Cengage Company

GALE
A Cengage Company

Farmington Hills, Mich • San Francisco • New York • Waterville, Maine
Meriden, Conn • Mason, Ohio • Chicago

Copyright © 2019 by Cindy Woodsmall and Erin Woodsmall.
All scripture quotations are from the King James Version of the Bible.
Thorndike Press, a part of Gale, a Cengage Company.

**LIBRARY OF CONGRESS CIP DATA ON FILE.
CATALOGUING IN PUBLICATION FOR THIS BOOK
IS AVAILABLE FROM THE LIBRARY OF CONGRESS**

ISBN-13: 978-1-4328-7008-9 (hardcover alk. paper)

Published in 2019 by arrangement with WaterBrook, an imprint of Random House, a division of Penguin Random House LLC

Printed in Mexico
1 2 3 4 5 6 7 23 22 21 20 19

To Mom: my second amazing mom.

*When you entered our lives, I was grown
with children of my own and so very sure
I didn't need another mom, so we
became friends instead. But now . . .
two decades later and forever . . .
you are Mom too. I learn from you. I vent
to you. I agree in prayer with you. But
most of all, in every good, healthy way,
I try to keep up with you.*

— Cindy

*To my children: Lucy, Caleb,
Silas, and Lincoln.*

*I hope your haven
will always be our family.*

*No matter how old or independent
you come to be, and when
adventures lead us far,
remember home is wherever we are.*
— Erin

ONE

Ivy placed the last of the pink-rose center-pieces on a crisp white tablecloth and paused to smell the fragrance of the soft petals. Vintage porcelain teapots held the arrangements, and on each table sat a three-tiered tray with chicken-salad finger sandwiches, pink and blue cupcakes, and chocolate-covered strawberries. The teapots looked so much happier now than when she had found them languishing in an old storage room of this Victorian home.

She smiled. What a beautiful setup for a party. Stacy, the mom-to-be, would be thrilled. A good recommendation from Stacy's family would help Ivy and Tegan get their fledgling party-planning business off the ground. She looked around the room and saw a few family members of the mom-to-be who had come to help Ivy with the preparations.

"Ivy?" Tegan pointed at the empty punch

bowl. "Should I go ahead and fill the bowl with the punch?"

Ivy glanced at the clock. "I'd give it ten more minutes. We don't want our punch-flavored ice melting too quickly."

Tegan nodded and returned her attention to the table in front of her.

Sunlight filtered through a stained-glass window, highlighting something on the rug. Ivy walked over to pick it up, and as she bent to retrieve the piece of decorative paper, she felt the envelope of money in the hidden pocket in her apron shift. She'd put most of her life savings from cleaning houses into that envelope and shoved it into her pocket a few hours ago. She couldn't wait to hand off the money as a down payment on an apartment. Everything she longed for was coming together — establishing a party-planning business, getting a place to live with her friend Tegan, and leaving the confines of her Old Order Amish life.

But her *Mamm's* sweet face flashed in her mind's eye, and she swallowed hard. The look in Mamm's eyes bored into her. The money wasn't freeing. It was heavy and dirty.

She straightened her shoulders. No. Today wasn't about guilt or fear. It was about chasing her dreams.

A giggle caught Ivy's attention, and she glanced at the six-year-old who'd arrived with her mom, grandma, and aunt and had been helping them set up tables. During the next twenty minutes, the rest of the guests would start trickling in.

Ivy smiled. "Thanks for your help, Lily. Are you excited about celebrating your new cousin?"

The girl nodded, her blue eyes sparkling and her long, curly brown hair bouncing with each movement. "Yes, yes, yes! I really want to eat *that* pink cupcake." She pointed at one of the nearby dessert trays. "And then Aunt Stacy said I could help her open all the gifts. Did you know that babies make big messes and go through lots of clothes?"

Tegan walked over from the table she'd just finished, dusted off her hands, and then smoothed her knee-length mauve lace dress. "Yeah, I have a little brother who was born when I was about your age, and I can confirm that."

Ivy nodded and grinned at the young girl. "You're pretty sharp."

Lily looked Ivy up and down. "Do the Amish have parties for babies?"

"Well, sort of. But not like this. Usually women take homemade gifts and clothes to the mom after the baby is born."

What Ivy didn't say was how quiet the Amish were about pregnancy, an odd practice in her book. She loved helping the *Englisch* create such beautiful celebrations. The Amish would consider today's event extravagant, with too much focus on an expectant mom. But no need to let Lily in on all that.

"Well, you should tell them it's fun. Or I can tell them for you." Lily gave a thumbs-up.

Tegan shrugged and pushed her long brown hair behind her shoulder. "Guess she's solved your problems."

Ivy forced a smile. If only it were that easy to change the minds of men and women who were convinced that following an old set of rules was the way to live. Most were reluctant to make a big deal about birthdays or any other special occasion except wedding days. Why weren't all kinds of milestones honored? Some special events should be celebrated in such a way that they become a lifetime memory. The common Amish practice of ignoring or, at most, having a low-key observance of important days grated on her nerves, to put it mildly.

"Wow, look at this place. It's beautiful!" Clara, the seventy-something owner of the

Victorian-era home, walked into the dining room. Her eyes moved from floor to ceiling, taking in the draped pink and blue tulle and fairy lights. She turned a slow circle as she looked around. "Truly beautiful." She smiled at Ivy. "Now's a good time for me to talk if you have a moment."

Tegan mouthed, "Good luck."

"Sure." Ivy waved to Lily and Tegan and followed Clara into the kitchen. The second floor of the spacious old house had been converted into an apartment with two bedrooms, a full bath, and a kitchenette. Clara lived in part of the main floor. The tenants had full use of the big kitchen except when the beautiful dining room was rented out for special events like today's baby shower. Ivy's heart raced a few beats. Would Clara let Tegan and her move into the upstairs apartment? If Clara decided to post the vacancy, she'd definitely get other applicants who actually had things like credit and a job history that consisted of more than dairy farming and cleaning houses. Tegan had the credit and the job history, but she didn't have the money for the down payment without her parents' help. And Clara likely thought, as many Englisch did, that since Amish young people didn't have a credit score, credit card, or job history outside the Amish community, that renting to someone Amish was a risk.

Clara sat in a chair at the small round table in the kitchen's sunny breakfast nook and gestured for Ivy to join her. She folded her crinkly hands in front of her on the table. "I've been thinking about your offer. I do want you and Tegan to live here. I really do. You both would be wonderful tenants, and God is my witness that I'm ready for nice girls to share my home with me. But I have concerns."

Ivy nodded and leaned forward, trying to calm the butterflies in her stomach.

Clara gave a half smile. "With her good credit Tegan has met the prequalifications I require, and her parents paid her first and last months' rent. Of course you don't have all those things, and I'm okay with that. I understand. But Tegan's parents have said it's a sink-or-swim time for their daughter, and we both know she can't afford the apartment without you. What I need you to know is that I cannot live on half of what that apartment is worth. I need the money from paying tenants to cover my living expenses. Without that money it'll be a struggle to afford heat come winter."

She wouldn't let Clara down. "Yes, that makes sense. I promise that paying the rent won't be an issue. Our party business is small right now, in part because of all I can't do to help Tegan grow it while I'm living Amish. But once we're here, we'll be able to throw all our energy into expanding the business, and, if need be, I can supplement my income with my old, faithful job of cleaning houses."

"I'm glad to hear you say that. I thought you felt strongly about living here. I would be thrilled if you and Tegan moved into the upstairs apartment after the current tenants move out in October."

They are moving out in four months? Ivy struggled to take a breath. The last she'd heard, the tenants were staying through the first of the year. Still, Clara was willing to accept Ivy as a tenant. A grin tugged at the corners of her mouth. "Really?"

"Of course, dear. You're such a bright spot in the day, and you always make people smile. I'd love to have you as part of this home."

Ivy's heart warmed. "That's great to hear. I brought my portion of the down payment."

Tegan was going to be so excited. She couldn't wait to get out of her not-so-safe neighborhood. They could live in this beautiful home and work on their business. And

Ivy would be available to pop in and check on Clara if she needed her. She enjoyed the sweet woman's company.

Ivy looked at the delicate lace curtains adorning the window by the table. Mamm's windows at home would never be decorated like this. *Mamm.* She was going to be crushed. But their relationship could mend in time, couldn't it? For years they had worked side by side, whether cleaning homes or milking cows, talking long into the night, laughing until their sides hurt.

The nagging questions returned: *Is it right to move into an Englisch home, even one as beautiful as this? Does my desire to do so make me ungrateful for the family and life I was given?*

Ivy pushed the thoughts aside. She reached into her dress pocket and pulled out the envelope. She'd managed to put back a few dollars from every house-cleaning job for the last two years. Inside the envelope was one thousand dollars in cash. It was hard to let go of so much money when Mamm and she were barely making ends meet, but she had to be brave. Her dreams were worth it, right?

She slid the envelope across the table to Clara.

Clara smiled. "I'm looking forward to your

moving in here."

Ivy's heart skipped as she rose from the chair. "*Denki,* Clara. I best get back to my work."

The rest of the afternoon was a blur. The party went off without a hitch, but Ivy found her good mood faltering here and there. Mamm would eventually understand, right?

After cleaning up and bidding farewell to everyone, she called a driver to take her home. She usually drove a horse and carriage to get where she needed to go. Sometimes Tegan gave her a ride, but neither of those were available today. For the first time in a month, the traveling blacksmith was coming by the farm to shoe the horses, so she was without a rig, and Tegan was meeting up with friends in town.

The June sun wasn't about to set, but she'd barely make it home in time for the evening milking. Thankfully she had eaten some of the sandwiches at the party, which should sustain her through the two hours of chores this evening.

The car rushed past the beauty of homes and farms that dotted the countryside. Some of the farmland was no longer used, abandoned through foreclosures or sitting idle because dairy cows had been sold and milking parlors had shut down. The over-head on a dairy farm often exceeded what could be earned. Cows were costly to feed, and vet bills were nonstop.

More than ten years ago, not long after *Daed* died, Mamm "loaned" most of their herd to dairy-farming relatives. That reduced the workload as well as the overhead so they were manageable, but it also meant that no milk broker would take the time to pick up their small amount of milk. The farm would've gone under had it not been for the Troyers, an Amish family who used to live just over the hill from them. After the Troyers lost their dairy farm, they moved closer to town and started a new business — making specialty cheeses and yogurts. Their business continued to grow, and they depended on Mamm for their milk.

But did Mamm really expect to continue to run the dairy farm year after year with just Ivy to help her? They had only ten cows. Some were in various stages of being a dry cow and couldn't be milked because they were pregnant or had a new calf that needed their milk. So Mamm and she milked only eight of the cows most months, but all the prep work and cleanup still required two hours every morning and every evening.

After Ivy exited the car and waved to the driver, she saw Mamm walking to the barn, just as she had done every morning and evening for the past ten and a half years. How long did Mamm want to keep this up? At fifty her health was great. But Ivy's sister, Holly, was marrying this December. Her brother, Red, lived in another town and was courting a girl he would marry. Neither of her siblings would live on this farm or even be close enough to help much.

"Ivy." Mamm's cheery voice washed over her as they embraced, but rather than Ivy feeling the usual comfort, knots formed in the pit of her stomach. "How was the job today, sweetie?"

"They loved it."

She wanted to share the details of the beautiful flowers, lace doilies, and fine china, but she held back. Mamm mucked stalls and sloshed through manure and mud to complete tasks she took pride in. Between milking cows in the morning and evening, she cleaned homes, often on her hands and knees, scrubbing away other people's filth. She asked about Ivy's job because she loved Ivy, not because she understood or even wanted to. Not really.

"Of course they did." Mamm squeezed her shoulder, and as Ivy followed her into the milking parlor, the familiar aroma of hay and cows hit her.

Mamm had spent years hoping Ivy's love of useless dainty things — from fine china to electric twinkly lights intertwined with colorful tulle — would be overshadowed by something with more substance. After all, Ivy's sister had a heart for what really mattered — working at a pharmacy and helping the Amish stay healthy.

As much as Ivy loved and respected Mamm, she couldn't stay. The Old Ways weren't for her. With the exception of their common faith in God and His Son, Ivy thought differently on a lot of topics the Amish held dear. How could she stay inside a strict society she didn't agree with?

Mamm climbed the ladder to the hayloft, not missing a beat even as she hoisted herself over a broken rung. Ivy kept intending to fix that. It was just one of dozens of things that needed repairing in the barn and milking parlor. But they never had any time it seemed. Still, despite all that needed repair, the structure itself — beams, trusses, stud walls, and foundation — was solid.

Ivy stood aside while Mamm tossed down the first bale of straw, and it landed with a thud. Ivy picked it up and tossed it next to the first stall. She and Mamm had this dance down pat after so many years. Prepare the stalls with straw, and fix the cows' post-milking meal of silage and hay. Let the first group of cows in, put on disposable latex gloves to prevent spreading mastitis and spreading germs to the cows, clean the teats with a predip iodine solution, dry them with a towel, strip the foremilk, attach milking machines as soon as the solution dried, clean the teats again after the milking, and finally treat the animals to their dinner. The whole process had to happen twice. Since they had only enough milking machines and working stalls for four of the presently eight milking cows, the whole process took longer.

Didn't Mamm ever dream about being done with this part of her life?

After the first set of cows were milked and cleaned, Ivy grabbed two pitchforks off the barn wall. She passed one to Mamm, who would put hay and grain in the trough again while Ivy put another layer of fresh straw in each stall. *Just tell her.* She hated keeping secrets from her Mamm. Doing so had been eating at her insides for two months.

"I . . . Well, there's no easy way to tell you this." *Say it.* "I put a payment down on a room at Clara's."

Mamm's pitchfork fell to the ground with a thud. She stared at Ivy. "What?"

Ivy's throat suddenly felt dry. "I want to move out. Um . . ." She swallowed. "I *am* moving out . . . in October."

Mamm gave a slow blink and then bent down to pick up her pitchfork. She stabbed at a bale of hay and shoved it into the feeding trough with a little too much force and then repeated the motion. Was she going to say anything?

Ivy noticed the cinder block they used to shore up the leaks in the cows' water trough was askew and too much water was leaking out. She knelt down to push it back into place.

Hyperstripe, Ivy's favorite gray-striped barn cat, hopped on top of the block and rubbed her face against Ivy's, purring. She wanted a milk sample, but Ivy gently nudged her aside.

Was the conversation with her Mamm really over for tonight?

"Why?" Mamm's singular word rang louder in Ivy's brain than the dropped pitchfork.

Ivy stood. "There are things I long to accomplish that can't be done if I stay under Amish rule. It's not you. I love you, but I have dreams. Really big ones. You know that, don't you?"

Mamm stopped stabbing at the hay. "What

I know is, our way of life is worth every rule. You think this is about who you are, but I know it boils down to your dreams of party planning. You need to make your dreams line up with the Old Ways. That's how our people have lived for hundreds of years."

How could Mamm be so dismissive? "Like Holly's dreams did?"

Holly was educated, was still in school actually, *and* had been baptized into the faith, which was unheard-of among the Amish. And her education, as well as her Englisch position at the pharmacy, had been sanctioned by the bishop.

Mamm's eyes opened wide. "Is that what this is about? Your sister broke through the rules, and you feel you deserve to do that also? If so, there's no comparison here, Ivy. Your sister gained special permission in order to provide much-needed medical advice to our people about their prescriptions and need for medication."

"No. She gained special permission to be her real self and follow her heart's desire. It just so happens that what she longed for was beneficial to the physical health of the Amish community, so the bishop agreed to it."

The hurt in Mamm's eyes was undeniable. Was Ivy being selfish? Hadn't she given up years of going her own way in order to support this family and the farm? "Mamm, I love you. You're an amazing Mamm, but I've been searching my heart for a while now, and the Amish way doesn't fit with who I am."

Did Mamm have tears in her eyes? Mamm took a deep breath. "You just want freedom to run off with Tegan and plan parties. All this time I thought it was just a hobby."

"That's not what this is about."

Her Mamm stared at her.

"It's not, Mamm. It's a symptom. If I have a cold, sneezing isn't the cause. It's a symptom of the real issue. A party-planning business is run out of the home. Connecting with clients requires a computer and internet access and spending a lot of time doing social media. I need to be able to fill rooms with supplies that include bolts of tulle and silky fabrics, twinkly electric lights, bins of lace tablecloths, china, and helium tanks to fill colorful balloons draped with ribbons. The list goes on and on, and none of that includes the hours I need on the internet. Clients need to be able to tell me the kind of music they prefer, and I need to be able to listen to music for hours while devising a playlist for the party. But none of that is the issue. Those are just symptoms.

The real issue is this life doesn't free me to be me. I *am* tulle and lace and twinkly lights, Mamm. But every single day I put on plain clothes, and twice a day I work for hours in muck in this barn as if that's who I am. If our people knew who I was, they'd be done with me, so I pretend, and I can't keep pretending."

"Living the Old Ways doesn't come natural for young people. I'll give you that. But it's not a matter of pretending. It's sacrificing our frivolous desires in order to pursue what really matters. The world offers ease and fun, but the Amish are a strong community with a durable faith, and nothing the world has can compare to that, not in the long run."

Mamm wasn't going to hear her, which seemed odd. She had listened well to Holly and Red, but Ivy's pleas were falling on deaf ears. It was time to draw this conversation to a close.

"Look, Mamm, I can still clean homes with you if you'll allow it" — she looked at the line of cows chewing their hay — "but I can't work this farm forever."

"You're talking nonsense. If I sold the cows and rented the barn to a nearby farmer, I think we'd still be having this conversation." Mamm clicked her tongue.

"As it happens, I talked to Red yesterday, and he said he's been thinking about coming back home. He'll free you of needing to help milk cows."

Regardless of what her brother said that sounded as if he might return, he wouldn't. He had a good job and a girl in Rocks Mill. He'd moved there more than a year ago to be closer to his girlfriend. Now he worked for her Daed, and her whole family had latched onto Red. He'd been home only once since he left. He wasn't moving back.

Ivy spread straw in the last of the four stalls. "It'll be nice when he comes home for another visit, Mamm. He's good help during those times." She would leave it at that, and Mamm could read between the lines. Holly helped most mornings, probably five out of seven days, but with her classes toward her licensed practical nurse degree and working at the pharmacy, her evenings were too busy. In six months she'd be married and gone.

Mamm scooped grain out of the bin and tossed it into the trough over the hay. "Ivy, what are you thinking? You want to leave your family — and your faith — for a fancy apartment?"

"No." Why did leaving the Amish have to equate to losing one's faith? "I have faith,

24

and I'm not losing it. And it's not about any one thing. It's about everything life could be if . . ."

"If" — Mamm's hand trembled as she wiped her sweaty brow — "you were free of the rules."

The conversation was circular. What could she say to help her Mamm understand? "Forget the rules. I'm trying to tell you the Amish ways aren't my ways. Holly and Red followed their hearts wherever their hearts led them, and I'm asking you to understand that I need to do the same."

"Their hearts did not lead them to forsake their heritage, an ancestry that many Amish died for in the beginning. Even when I was a girl, Amish men went to jail for taking a stand against the government, which was trying to make us do things their way. What we have as Amish people is precious and worth the sacrifice. Can't you see that?"

Ivy's heart ached. Her mother would never understand and never accept Ivy's decision.

"I suppose this is my fault." Mamm leaned her pitchfork against the wall and walked toward the second set of cows.

"Fault?" Ivy followed her.

Mamm pulled on a fresh pair of latex gloves. "It's what everyone will think and say, and it's the truth. I've raised you too worldly. I allowed too many things to make your life easier after your Daed passed. I hired a driver to take you back and forth to school, and I let you become close to our Englisch neighbors. Being friends with Tegan helped you through your grief after your Daed died. I should've realized what kind of influence that would have on a twelve-year-old."

"There's no fault here, Mamm. Our lives were forever changed when Daed died, and we all did what we could to survive it." Ivy pulled on a new set of gloves. "Including all it took to keep this dairy farm functioning. But we're not at that place anymore. Why do you want to keep doing all this?" She gestured to the cows.

"It's your Daed's family's farm. It's where I'm supposed to be. He wouldn't want me to sell it." Mamm picked up a container of the predip iodine solution.

"Are you sure? He'd want you to be happy. Red and Emily will probably marry soon. And we know Holly and Joshua are going to wed in December. What if you sold this farm and moved in with one of them or at least rented a home nearby? They're going to have your grandkids. You'd be in a home full of new life. Not on an old dairy farm with your single daughter, working too many hours each day."

Mamm set down the container of predip and turned to look at Ivy. "I would work this farm every day by myself for the rest of my life if it meant you staying Amish. This is going to break everyone's heart. It's breaking mine just to think of you leaving. And it could cause serious problems for your sister."

"How so?"

"If you leave our community before Holly gets married, how will her new bishop feel about her plan to continue working at Greene's Pharmacy? Her sister gone into the world, and she's asking to work full time as a married woman? It'll be hard enough as it is."

Oh. Ivy hadn't considered that. "Mamm, I'm sorry. I didn't think about that, but —"

"Of course you didn't think about it. You're moving too fast. All of this is too fast. Did you sign your name to a contract?"

"No, but —"

"Good. That settles it. Nothing happens until after the first of the year. Maybe by then you'll come to your senses."

Just how old did her Mamm think she was? At twenty-three she didn't need her Mamm's permission. She'd promised Clara that paying on time wouldn't be a problem. "I can't wait until then. I gave my word. Daed always said that's just as binding as a contract." She didn't make enough money from milking cows to cover each month's rent. But she could make enough from party planning *if* she was free to give her time to that instead of this farm.

"You shouldn't have entered into any agreement before talking to me. Go back to that woman and tell her that *if* you move in, it won't be until January." Mamm picked up the predip again and headed toward the second set of cows. "Fix this, Ivy."

How could she possibly return to Clara and ask to change the move-in date to January? Clara said she needed the money for her livelihood. Clara and Tegan were depending on Ivy to keep her word.

No. She wouldn't do that to either of them.

But if she left months before Holly's wedding, would it ruin her sister's chance of getting married?

She hadn't banked on her Mamm feeling this betrayed. It was as if the foundation of their relationship was cracking under Ivy's feet like the ice-skating pond in late winter.

Could she actually leave and break her

Mamm's heart? Could she stay and break her own?

Two

Darkness surrounded Arlan as he climbed the ladder to the hayloft. He hadn't slept much of late for thinking about his sister. She'd been sick to her stomach day and night for weeks. Did she have some strange virus or cancer?

The sounds of the wee hours of the morning — crickets, a barn owl, and tree frogs — were comforting. A cow lowed softly from somewhere nearby. The Keim farm would come alive with busyness in an hour or two, but this was his time. Everyone else in his house was fast asleep, and he had some guilt-free time to sink into another world.

He lit a kerosene lamp, knelt next to the hiding spot, and removed several loose boards. Every time he came here to read, he kept the wick in the lamp short so it didn't give off much light, and he hid the light behind strategically placed bales of hay. A warm June breeze swept through the barn loft. He pulled out *The Count of Monte Cristo,* sat on the roughhewn flooring, and leaned against a hay bale. This spot wasn't much for comfort, but it was quiet here and secretive, a place to enjoy the forbidden fruit of reading something other than the Bible. Years ago he'd found five old books in a trash bin behind a grocery store while waiting on his Mamm. He'd hidden them under the seat in the carriage, and he'd been hiding them in this loft ever since. Swartzentruber Amish and fiction did not mix at all, at least not out in the open. Arlan couldn't be the only Swartzentruber person to secretly read fiction.

He opened the book but couldn't tune out concern for his sister. Why was she so sickly, and why were she and Mamm crying so much these days? He'd asked Magda twice when he thought no one was around but was interrupted by either Mamm or Daed. He shoved those thoughts aside and read the words before him. Soon he was pulled into that world — a prison cell in a concrete fortress surrounded by water.

A creaking sound grabbed Arlan's attention. Had the barn door just opened and shut?

"Your tears have to stop, Mary Ella." The

firm voice belonged to his Daed. "Enough is enough. No amount of crying will undo what your oldest daughter has done."

What had Magda done? Swartzentruber Amish had far fewer freedoms than any other sect of the Amish. Unlike the Old Order Amish, the Swartzentruber Amish didn't allow their youth a *rumschpringe* because they considered a time of running around to be sinful.

Arlan didn't dare budge. His Daed was in no mood to discover the reason Arlan was often in the barn in the mornings before anyone else. It wouldn't matter to his Daed that he was twenty-two — only that he was disobeying by reading fiction.

"I'm trying to stop. I am." His Mamm broke into fresh sobs.

"We're doing the right thing," Daed said.

"What if we're found out?"

"We won't be. We can't be." His Daed sounded staunch but also desperate.

"I know it has to be done." His Mamm's voice cracked. "But Magda is so upset with us. She wants to raise the baby herself."

Raise the baby? Arlan couldn't breathe. *What?* That made no sense. At only seventeen Magda had never courted, and the Swartzentruber Amish didn't allow any kind of nonsense that would provide unsupervised time between single men and women.

"She will settle down, and it will help her do so if you stop crying every time she does," Daed said. "But she's refused to answer my question. Is it possible she doesn't know who the father is?"

"She knows," Mamm said. "I saw it in her eyes."

"Englisch then." His Daed clicked his tongue the way he did whenever he was disappointed in his offspring, which was often. "We stick to the plan, and one day when she's marrying a good man, she'll thank us."

A thudding sound caused the barn to go completely silent. Arlan looked out the open doors of the barn loft and saw that his youngest brother had come out of their home and was entering the outhouse. His parents left the barn, hurrying toward the house.

Arlan looked at the night sky with its glory of stars. Memories of growing up with Magda made a pitchfork jab his heart. He was the second oldest of eight, but he and Magda had the closest bond. How he longed to hear her laugh and see the hope that used to dance in her eyes.

The starry view in front of him was so peaceful. Should he just pretend he didn't know the truth?

He put the book back in its hiding place, his mind spinning. Mamm was always sick when another brother or sister was on the way. That had to be what was going on with Magda. But was Mamm ever this sick?

He descended the ladder, and rather than going inside the house, he decided to start on his chores. It was about that time anyway.

As he cleaned and then milked each cow by hand, the conversation he'd heard stayed on his mind. *She wants to raise the baby herself.*

What were his parents planning for Magda? And there was an Englisch father? When would Magda have been around the Englisch?

Then it hit him like a punch to the gut. He'd been the one to introduce Magda to Rodney, an Englischer about Arlan's age, who was saving for college while managing a local shop. Rodney had been listing Magda's homemade candles for sale online and in the shop, and Magda was able to use the electricity in the shop to heat the paraffin. Arlan's instincts had said it was a bad idea to get mixed up in a business venture with non-Swartzentrubers, but he and Magda were so desperate to earn money that he'd ignored his better judgment.

His twenty-year-old brother, Elam, joined

34

him for the milking. Their Daed didn't help them, but sometimes he tended to other duties.

After he and Elam finished milking and feeding the herd and storing the milk, Arlan went down the hill to the small stream that ran behind the family's farm to wash the grime off his arms and face. If his parents were trying too hard to hide what was happening with Magda, could he help her in a way she needed while following his order's rules?

He pressed cool water against his eyes and let his mind wander.

When most of the Pennsylvania Swartzentrubers had moved to New York two years ago, Arlan had longed to follow. The church there was less strict than here, and his girlfriend, Lorraine, was there, waiting for him. His older brother, Nathaniel, had moved to New York with the other families, and Arlan had invested good money in his brother's farm. Nathaniel needed his help, but Daed had said that he couldn't lose his two oldest sons at the same time and that Arlan could leave when his younger brother Elam turned twenty-one. That was only six months from now. Arlan had spent the last year and a half working, saving money, writing letters to Lorraine, and dreaming of joining the New York Swartzentruber community.

For as far back as Arlan could remember, he'd longed to know God better, to have a family of his own, and to work a dairy farm. Waiting for Elam to turn twenty-one seemed a small price to pay for the right to marry and to be part owner — although a very small part — of a farm.

He slung water from his hands and meandered back toward the house. Based on the sun's position, he knew the family would be eating breakfast soon. His stomach growled. Was Magda eating? She'd been absent from every meal for a week. Shouldn't his parents be more concerned?

Arlan entered the white clapboard house with its faded blue trim and walked toward the kitchen. He heard the usual chatter of voices from his younger sisters as they and Mamm worked to put breakfast on the table. Daed and Elam were already sitting at the table.

He sat, and after the silent prayer his Daed began putting food on his plate and passing the dish to Arlan. Including Magda, Arlan had six younger siblings. How did the room feel so empty with only Magda missing?

Arlan dipped corn porridge and scrambled eggs onto his plate. His Mamm set a mug of coffee with milk in front of him. He swallowed a few bites, but despite his hunger the food felt heavy going down, and the coffee was bitter on his tongue. He had to say *something*.

"Magda's still not well enough to eat?"

Mamm and Daed made eye contact with each other. "Not yet."

Mamm pointed upward. "But she's resting a lot. I expect she'll be up and about one day soon."

Was anyone going to state the obvious? "Don't you think it's time we take her to a doctor?"

"No, that's not what she needs," Mamm said.

Daed scooped another bite of eggs with his fork. "We're taking care of Magda. This doesn't concern you, son."

"But she's not eating. We'd treat a sick animal if it was acting poorly."

Daed set down his fork and put both hands on the tabletop. "You don't understand. And I told you this isn't your business." Daed's tone said the conversation was over.

Arlan had been tempted many times to push back when his Daed gave his final word on a matter, but he never had. The Word made no bones about obeying one's parents. "Daed, is this the way it will be?"

Daed's brows furrowed. "Meaning?"

"With Magda. She's not eating, not well enough to join us for meals. If she's still this sick in a week, will you feel any different about getting help?"

"Maybe God is judging her, and we won't interfere."

"So she's made her bed, and now she can sleep in it. Is that it?" Arlan could remember Daed repeating that saying a thousand times over the years, even when Arlan and his siblings were trying to obey but made a mistake or something happened by accident.

"That's right and more than you need to know."

What was their plan, the one that Magda was crying over and refusing to agree with? Arlan pushed his wooden chair back as he stood, the chair legs scraping the floor. "I'm at least going to take her some food."

"Fine, but you say nothing about going to a doctor. A little pain and suffering will set her straight. Besides, running off to a doctor for every little thing isn't our way. You know that."

Arlan looked at Daed, but he didn't reply. Oh, he knew their way well. No doctors unless an emergency. No rumschpringe. No indoor plumbing. No rugs. No flashlights. No phone on the property. The *no* list seemed endless. And parents have the final say in all things until their children marry.

If Arlan could just stick it out until Elam turned twenty-one, he'd have his Daed's blessing and could move to New York. Without Daed's blessing he wouldn't be welcome to join the New York Swartzentrubers. Once there, he and Lorraine could earn the trust of the bishop and marry. Then he'd have his own life. But how could he leave Magda?

He stood and spooned some breakfast onto a plate. Maybe Magda could eat a few bites. The only time anyone in the family had seen a doctor was at a local clinic, and it mostly had midwives and a nurse who prescribed antibiotics for ear infections or bronchitis. He couldn't take Magda there or to the medicine store without it getting back to Mamm and Daed. The only other place he knew about was an emergency room where Daed had gone when he almost severed a finger. They'd hired a driver to get there. Should he take Magda there? He could drive a horse and buggy without raising suspicion, but he didn't know where the hospital was. And he wasn't sure how much care she could receive there without her parents' permission since she was under eighteen. Suddenly he remembered another place. A different medicine store that his Old Order neighbor had mentioned once.

He carried the plate of food upstairs to Magda's room and tapped on the door.

"Kumm rei." Her voice was soft.

The old door creaked as he opened it. Magda was sitting in a wooden rocking chair with a small metal pail in her lap. When she looked up, the thinness of her face shook him. Dark smudges framed her brown eyes, and her lips were pale and chapped. She cringed when she saw the plate in his hands and shook her head. Was the sight of food that repulsive?

He took a step into the room. "Magda, you need to eat."

"I can't. Not that stuff at least. I've been able to eat a few crackers here and there and drink lemonade. I can at least keep that down sometimes. But please get that out of here." She gagged.

Arlan walked out of the room and set the plate on the floor to the side of the door. Then he went back inside, closing the door behind him. He crossed the room, pulled up a footstool, and sat close, facing her. "How much food and drink did you have yesterday?"

"Three crackers and a few sips of lemonade."

Was this all the food she was taking in each day? "That doesn't sound like enough."

Magda shook her head. "It doesn't feel like enough, but it's all I can manage."

The memory of a ten-year-old Magda handing him a brown bag flashed in his mind. He'd been fifteen and had gotten into a patch of poison ivy while clearing some brush from their land, and it'd blistered badly. Daed determined that the rash wasn't worth any medicine, but during outdoor chore time while Mamm was weeding the garden, Magda slipped off and cut through fields and woods to walk to a gas station. She used her own money to buy him calamine lotion and cortisone ointment.

And she'd said, *"Promise me, Arlan, that we'll always take care of each other, no matter what. Even if Mamm and Daed are being unfair and won't listen."*

He closed his eyes and thought of Lorraine: her beautiful eyes sparkling in the evening light during their last buggy ride the night before she and her family left for New York. If he helped Magda, would he jeopardize his standing in the community? Would that cause Lorraine to think less of him, maybe not want to marry him? Fear twisted around his desire to help Magda. He clenched his fists, trying to dispel its power.

He opened his eyes and looked at his sister. "I'm taking you to get some medicine. I'm not sure how much longer you can survive like this."

"You'd do that for me? I'm not worth —"

"You are." Regardless of what had gotten her into this situation, it could never change his love for her and her worth both to him and to God. She could seek forgiveness after she was better. And he could too. "Look, to do this, to get you out of here, you have to be willing to disobey Mamm and Daed. Are you willing to do that?"

She gave a slow nod. "*Ya*, but you've always followed what Daed said."

The weight of his decision to disobey bore down hard. He'd been an obedient son, but after all his years of doing as he was told, had Daed's heart softened one bit when Arlan asked to get help for Magda? *Nee.* Maybe his obedience had given Daed an unobstructed path for complete control.

"How?" Magda searched his eyes. "I wouldn't put it past them to create a wall of men to stop us."

She wasn't exaggerating, but he had to

42

find a way. "I don't know. Give me a few days. We'll find answers, I promise."

The medicine store . . . What did the Englisch call it? A pharmacy, and the one his neighbor had mentioned kept popping into his mind. Did it mean that was where he needed to go? The name had a color in it. Perhaps green. He'd need to get directions and details, but he seemed to remember it was less than an hour away by horse and buggy. He could get her there somehow. Maybe he needed to hire a driver.

Magda's hands trembled as she brushed hair off her face. "I need more than medicine, Arlan. I need a way out."

"Out?" Arlan whispered. *What had Mamm said? She wants to raise the baby herself? Do they intend to make her give the baby away?*

Magda gagged and clasped a wet washrag over her mouth. "Out." Her head fell back against the chair, and her breathing was labored. "Do you understand?" she mumbled through the cloth.

"I'm starting to, ya." His mind spun with ideas, and his heart pounded as if it were trying to leave his chest. He had a few thousand dollars saved. "Okay. We'll leave together and then give Daed time to cool off and become reasonable. That might take a while."

Once she had medicine to stop her from throwing up, they could head north. He was able-bodied and skilled at dairy farming. About ten years ago he'd worked for an Englisch neighbor, helping on his dairy farm, and the man had talked about dairy farms north of them. Arlan had learned a lot about farming the Englisch way, so maybe he could get a job on one of those farms, although his Daed had never permitted him to go inside an Englisch home.

He could call home in a few months to see if his parents would let Magda keep the baby. If they refused, he and Magda wouldn't return until after the baby was born. Then they would beg for forgiveness and work hard to make things right with their parents, church leaders, and district.

Would the new Swartzentruber community in New York welcome him after hearing he had disobeyed his parents?

Did it matter?

He had to do this for his sister.

THREE

Ivy hummed an Englisch song over the *clippety-clop* of her horse's hooves and the grind of the rig's wheels. The song had been stuck in her head all morning. She kept her voice low enough that her passengers couldn't hear.

Where had she heard that song? Perhaps on the radio at Greene's Pharmacy. Lyle, the owner, had good taste in music. Maybe she would hear the tune while cleaning the pharmacy after she and Holly went out to lunch, but first she had to drop off two sweet young friends — Dora and Eva. She'd miss seeing them after she moved out, but hopefully by then she would have made sure Eva had the medical help she needed.

Holly would approve of that, at least.

Thoughts of Mamm crowded in, and Ivy no longer felt like humming. Her Mamm was one of a kind, and she deserved for Ivy to honor her, but did that mean Ivy needed to give her life over to her Mamm's faith? Ivy had wrestled with herself for years, trying to fit her round-peg thinking into a square-peg world. But she'd lost the battle. Still, she could figure out a way to change her move-out date for Mamm, couldn't she?

How hurt would her sister be when Ivy left the Amish? Josh, her fiancé, was open-hearted, so Holly and Ivy could stay in contact and remain close. Even so, the thought of how Holly would feel washed more sadness over Ivy. Her decision wasn't against anyone personally, especially not her family. Far from it.

Someone tapped her shoulder, and she turned to smile at Dora. She and her sister Eva were as quiet as the first time Ivy had taken them to and from a cleaning job last fall. Maybe their silence was part of the way they were raised. Even though Ivy, Dora, and Eva were all Amish, Dora and Eva were Swartzentruber Amish. The differences, both large and subtle, between Old Order and Swartzentruber rules were numerous. In fact, it seemed to Ivy that the gulf between the two sects was wider than the distance between Old Order and Englisch.

Dora pointed to the next right. "That's the shortcut I was telling you about."

"Sure." Ivy pulled the reins to turn the

horse onto the dirt road Dora gestured to. "You girls did great work today."

Eva had completed her share of the work cleaning out an Old Order woman's craft storage building this morning, but Ivy had noticed the girl wheezing each time they'd worked together. Ivy had first met Eva and Dora when she saw them walking along the roadside and stopped to see if they needed a lift. Eva seemed to be struggling to breathe, but she assured Ivy she was fine. When Ivy asked Holly about it, Holly mentioned it was possible the girl had asthma.

Later Ivy asked the girls if they'd like to work for her Mamm's house-cleaning business, and they had agreed and were really hard workers. But was the girls' mother aware that medicines were available that might fix this issue? Ivy had shared information with the girls a few times and had sent info home with them, but Holly hadn't seen them at the pharmacy yet. Still, on the chance that one day their Mamm would ask about the medicine, Ivy kept a brochure for Greene's Pharmacy and a contact card for the Martel Clinic in her pocket whenever she picked up or dropped off the girls.

She turned the rig onto a dirt driveway and pulled up to the family's white farmhouse. Ivy signaled to her horse to stop. "Can I pick you up tomorrow, late morning? I have another job lined up, and I could use a few extra hands."

Eva nodded. "Denki."

As the girls exited the passenger side, their mother, Sarah, opened the door and was waving at Ivy to come in.

Progress!

She got out and tied her horse to the hitch.

"Will you come in for a moment and have a slice of banana bread and a cup of coffee?"

Ivy smiled. "I'd love to." Holly would forgive her if she ruined her appetite before their lunch.

Soon she was sitting at Sarah's table and making small talk. Dora and Eva sliced the bread and poured coffee for the women and then joined them at the table. Two toddler boys with straight blond hair cut just below their ears were peeking around the corner. Ivy smiled and waved at them, and they immediately ran off.

"Denki, Ivy. It's nice to have some pocket money for the girls. Many mouths to feed, you know."

Ivy nodded. Even though her own family was small, they'd faced many lean years despite working the dairy farm and also cleaning houses.

"Eva said there's medicine that might help her breathe easier."

"There is, but I don't know anything about it except that it exists. My sister, Holly, does though. How long has Eva's breathing been difficult?"

Sarah nibbled her lip and looked at the wall a moment before answering, "A year, maybe two. I almost took her to see a doc once, but it's so expensive, and I don't want our family to deal with the Englisch more than we have to. It's never so bad it's dangerous. She just has to slow down sometimes."

Ivy reached into her apron pocket. "This is the same information I sent home with the girls one time." She placed the Greene's Pharmacy brochure on the table and slid it toward the woman. "My sister works there, and I clean the front of the store. Holly has a passion to make sure the Amish are receiving proper health care. Greene's is not a typical pharmacy. They're sensitive, discreet, and give special pricing to Amish or anyone who can't afford to pay full price." She placed the Martel Clinic card next to the Greene's brochure. "And this clinic near the pharmacy is run by a friend. She's

Englisch, but she's kind and knows our ways."

Sarah took both items and stared at them. "I'll think about it."

"Just consider it, ya? I know you love your children and want the best for them. I think these people can help Eva."

"Maybe so."

Ivy finished her snack and thanked Sarah and her girls again.

Wouldn't Holly be excited if Eva got the needed help? It would be so good to see her young friend breathe easier.

After saying goodbye to the family, Ivy spent the forty-five minutes back to Raysburg thinking mostly about what Holly would say when she told her she was leaving the Amish. For months she'd been bursting at the seams to talk to Holly about leaving, to bare all to her sister. She and Holly had never kept secrets from each other. But Ivy had needed to work through this on her own, and now that she had a plan in place, Mamm had asked her not to tell Holly or anyone else until after the wedding. Could Ivy really keep something this big from her sister?

She hitched her horse in the field the Amish used to park their rigs and gave him some fresh oats. Then she crossed the street into the downtown area. The old-fashioned pharmacy came into view. Was the business doing better? Lyle, the owner, had suffered a stroke last fall, and Lyle's son, Brandon, had moved home and stepped up as the pharmacist-in-charge.

Tires screeched on a street nearby. How odd. Most drivers in Raysburg went slowly, accustomed as they were to the Amish, who drove on the same streets in horses and buggies. She looked up to see a gray, rusty car careening through downtown.

What on earth —

The car was veering back and forth, just missing scrambling pedestrians and cars parallel parked along the street. Ivy ran until she came to a building. She backed against it and had a street lamp and a parked car between her and the rogue vehicle.

They can't stop.

Her eyes tracked the car, time seeming to slow. Could the driver be aiming for the grassy field she'd come from? But just as the car seemed to be turning that way, a buggy coming toward the car blocked it, and the buggy's horse reared.

The gray car jerked the other way — straight into a glass window.

Greene's glass window.

Was this actually happening? *Please, God,*

let everyone be safe! Ivy sprinted to Greene's.

The beautiful antique front door and windows were smashed into shards of glass and wood. Pieces stuck out from the car's hood. The vehicle wasn't moving now.

"Holly!" Ivy stepped over some broken glass. She couldn't see anyone yet. *Please be safe!*

"I'm here. I'm okay. We're all okay." Her sister's voice was calm. "No one was in the front of the store."

Ivy tried to draw on Holly's peace and the consolation that customers and workers were safe. But what about the poor people inside the car? The car's windshield was shattered, but it wasn't collapsing on the passengers inside. For now.

"Are you okay?" she yelled to the driver as she looked in the side window, which was still intact. Her eyes widened. A young Amish man was the driver and, judging by his haircut and style of plain clothes, a Swartzentruber! His beard looked no older than a few days, but it was a sure sign he was married, either not for very long or, like a lot of the younger men, he couldn't grow much of a beard.

He was looking around as if he was trying to make sense of the situation. "Ya, I'm fine." His voice was muffled by the door, but his words were clear enough. He seemed to notice his passenger slumped against the opposite side window. "Help her. *Help* her!" He tried to reach her, but his seatbelt held him in place. He yanked on it, but it didn't budge.

Ivy ran past Lyle and to the opposite side of the car, but Brandon and Holly hurried there first. Ivy caught a glimpse of the woman slumped against the car door. She had on a Swartzentruber black bonnet, but since her head was tilted downward, Ivy couldn't see her face.

"Don't move her. She might be injured." Brandon looked down the road. "I called an ambulance, and it'll be here in minutes."

The woman sat up and wrapped her hands around her abdomen. Holly yanked the door open and knelt beside her, murmuring calm reassurances.

"Are you able to put the car in park and turn off the ignition?" Brandon asked the driver with the same calm tone Holly was using.

The woman was whispering to Holly in Pennsylvania Dutch. Ivy couldn't make out the young woman's words, but she knew desperation on someone's face when she saw it.

The young man nodded at Brandon. After finally freeing himself from the seatbelt, he slid the gearshift to park and turned the key. The struggling engine sputtered to silence.

He leaned over to his passenger. "I'm sorry. I'm so sorry."

"She says she doesn't think she's injured." Holly was squeezing the woman's hand. "But we need to have her checked by a doctor."

The woman rested her head on the driver's shoulder. "Arlan . . . all this to get medicine for me. What'll happen now?"

The man grimaced, leaning back against the headrest. "Just breathe," he whispered.

No one said anything for a few minutes, giving the couple time to adjust to their circumstances while waiting on the ambulance to arrive.

Brandon walked around to the driver's side. "I think I hear the ambulance now. The paramedics and EMTs will take great care of you and get you both to the hospital."

"No!" Both driver and passenger spoke at the same time.

The young Swartzentruber woman looked back and forth between Ivy and Holly, and Ivy could finally see her face.

"We can't . . . They'll find us. Please."

Was she still a minor? What could a young Swartzentruber couple be running from that they would attempt to drive a car?

Holly's eyes met Ivy's. It was clear these people were desperate. But to help these runaways could undermine all that Holly was doing to reach the Swartzentruber Amish community and their medical needs.

Ivy knelt next to Holly and put what she hoped was a comforting hand on the young woman's dress where it covered her leg.

The young man seemed to be holding his breath, waiting for an answer, and he hadn't budged to leave the car. Maybe he wouldn't until his passenger did.

Holly nodded at the girl. "Okay. No hospital for now."

"Seriously, Holly?" Brandon gestured at the wreckage.

Ivy stifled a sigh. Brandon didn't understand the Old Ways, especially the most conservative thinkers. "Brandon, these two won't agree to be seen at an Englischer hospital. We have to figure out another way."

Holly kept her eyes on the girl. "I have a good friend that is almost a doc, a reliable person who works with our communities and respects our ways. How about we go see her instead, ya? But I can't guarantee this won't end in a hospital visit."

Doc Jules was a nurse practitioner, and she'd be able to help. But who was this couple, and why were they so panicked?

FOUR

I hope this is the right decision. Holly guided the young woman into a patient room at the Martel Clinic. She had texted Julie to let her know they were coming, and the front staff let them through. But should they be at the hospital instead? Maybe Holly should've insisted the girl get in the ambulance that arrived a few minutes after the accident. Instead the EMTs on board collected a statement from Brandon and then left. The police remained. But Ivy was right. Neither Greene's nor the Martel Clinic had ever treated anyone from the ultraconservative Swartzentruber community, so how could they force them into the hospital against their will? And what would stop this woman from just leaving the hospital?

The man who was driving the car had to stay at the scene to talk to the police. Holly was confident Lyle wouldn't press charges. Not against a young couple obviously in desperate circumstances. But what was wrong with this poor young woman?

"It's going to be okay." Holly helped her settle into a chair. "What's your name?"

The girl shook her head. "Can't say." Without warning she stood, hurried to the sink, and leaned over it. She heaved as if she were going to vomit, but nothing came up. She took a few breaths. "I'm sorry," she whispered, her voice wavering. She returned to the chair and slunk into it.

Holly studied the young woman. Dry lips, sunken eyes, and no tears even when she was upset. If Holly were a betting person, she'd put money on the fact that the girl was dehydrated. Perhaps due to a nasty GI infection. Or maybe she was pregnant and was experiencing extreme nausea. The girl had clutched her stomach after the car crash.

"It's okay. I just want to help you. Can you tell me why you came to town?"

"I'm not feeling well." She took another set of fast breaths and looked focused, as if trying not to throw up. "We heard you have medicine that can help people and you'll keep it quiet."

"That's right." Holly pulled up the second chair in the room to sit in front of her. "What can I call you? You don't need to give me your last name right now, and you don't need to be afraid. I'm Holly."

The girl straightened her askew bonnet. "Magda."

The door to the patient room opened, and Julie stepped in.

"Hi there." Julie pulled the door closed behind her. "I'm Julie. I heard about what happened. I'm so sorry you've had such a rough day. Would you like for Holly to step out while we talk?"

Magda fiddled with her apron fabric. "Nee, I'm glad she's here."

Julie took another step into the room. "I'd like to take a look at you and assess you after the crash. Is that okay?"

Magda looked at Holly, questions flashing in her brown eyes.

"Julie is my doctor friend that I was telling you about at the crash."

"I'm not a doctor, though, but most Amish choose to call me Doc Jules."

Holly nodded. "She'll help you. And having Julie examine you is the only way to avoid going to the hospital after an accident like that."

"Okay."

Julie smiled. "Thank you for trusting me. I have one more request." She crossed the room to the exam table, opened a drawer underneath the bed part, and pulled out a folded gown. "I need you to put on this exam gown. It opens in the back so I can look at your spine and listen to your breathing."

Magda frowned. "You can't do what you need with me in my dress?"

There were so many things about medical visits that made them difficult for Amish patients. Had Magda never had a physical? Holly couldn't imagine growing up Swartzentruber and having to deal with all this. She took the dark-green gown from Julie and set it in Magda's lap. "The clinic had these gowns made special with Amish patients in mind. In most Englisch clinics they use paper gowns, and in the hospital they have thin cloth ones. This gown will keep you covered but will let Julie do her job. I wear one when I get my yearly physical."

"I know this is uncomfortable and you don't want this," Julie said, "but if your goal is to avoid the hospital, I need to make sure you're okay, and I can't do that through all these layers of clothing."

Magda nodded again. "Okay. Can I keep my *Kapp* on?"

"Yes, of course."

Holly waited while Magda stepped into

the attached bathroom to change into the gown, and when Magda returned, she helped her onto the exam table. Holly talked Magda through the examination in what she hoped were soothing tones while Julie checked head to toe for injuries from the crash. Before Julie could finish, she had to pause for Magda to dry heave.

When the exam was over, Julie draped her stethoscope around her neck. "Thank you, Magda. I'm not seeing any obvious injuries, although you might be sore tomorrow. More concerning, however, is that I believe you're dehydrated. It'll take a blood and a urine analysis to determine how severe, but your breathing and heart rate are faster than what is normal, and you have low blood pressure. Your body tried to throw up once during the exam. How many times a day has this been happening?"

Magda shrugged. "I don't know. A lot."

"And how many days have you been sick?"

"A few weeks. It's hard to remember."

Julie pulled up the swivel stool and took a seat next to the exam table so she could look Magda in the eye. "I need to ask a few hard questions. Are you pregnant?"

Magda looked at the floor. "Ya." Her voice was barely audible.

Holly rubbed Magda's shoulder. So one

61

of her guesses was right. Was this a pregnancy conceived outside of marriage? Perhaps that was Magda's reason for secrecy. But as difficult as that would be on a young couple, it wasn't so unusual that they'd need to flee their community and family.

"Thanks for telling me. Has anyone hurt you or done anything to you against your will?"

Magda was silent for a long moment.

Holly met Julie's eyes. Were they dealing with an abuse situation here?

Magda swallowed. "No, not that. No one has hurt me."

Julie took one of Magda's hands in hers. "If you ever need to share something, you can know that Holly and I, as medical professionals, are bound by laws that protect your confidentiality. Anything you tell us stays secret unless you give permission."

"Denki."

"With that information I'd like to start you on IV fluids and antinausea medicine. This means I'm going to put a needle in your hand" — Julie pointed to the back of her own hand — "and you'll receive fluids through a tube to replenish your body and medicine to stop your vomiting. Thankfully this clinic is equipped to do that. Then I'll need to run a few more tests and use our small but functional ultrasound machine to take pictures of your baby. Most likely your body is having a severe reaction to the pregnancy. It's rare but happens to some. Even the future queen of England has to be hospitalized every time she's pregnant."

Holly gave a reassuring smile. "They'll take good care of you here."

Julie nodded. "Just sit and relax, and I'll get a nurse to help me get those fluids going. Holly, a word, please?"

"I'll be right back." She patted Magda's shoulder and followed Julie to the hallway.

Julie pulled the door closed behind them. "I need to be honest. This makes me nervous."

"What does?" Surely they'd seen dehydrated patients in this clinic, or they wouldn't offer the IV fluids.

"Treating a pregnant patient with a probable diagnosis of hyperemesis gravidarum as an outpatient in this clinic. No one here is an ob-gyn, and more than one life is at stake. And even worse would be if we scan her with the ultrasound machine and find out a molar pregnancy is causing her to be so sick to her stomach."

"But if we send her to the hospital now, she could try to leave against medical advice. And if she disappeared, we'd lose

63

track of her because we have no information. You saw her reaction to your question about abuse. I don't know why she's running, but she's spooked. Spooked enough to arrive in a car with a Swartzentruber man driving. I don't think you understand how desperate they must be."

Julie tucked a stray strand of blond hair behind her ear. "I may not understand all the details, but I can tell she's scared. Still, if anything goes wrong, this clinic would be in huge trouble."

"I understand."

"Do you?" Julie held Holly's gaze. "Look, we can give her eight or so hours on fluids and antinausea meds until the clinic closes. But after that I need to see a big improvement, or I'll have no choice but to move her to the hospital. And that's assuming the other tests come back okay. It's not in her best interest to release her."

There had to be another option they could try. "How about if after the clinic closes, she comes to stay with me, Ivy, and Mamm? We can bring her back to the clinic first thing tomorrow morning."

"I can agree to that. At least that way I could drop by to check on her if need be, but" — Julie held up a finger — "with one addendum. Once the antinausea medicine

64

gets in her system, if she continues to dry heave, she has to go to a hospital. Understand?"

"I do." Holly had gone to bat for Magda's privacy. Unfortunately, if something bad happened, not only would Holly feel guilty forever, but Julie and the clinic could face real trouble. Did she make the right call? What if she didn't know until it was too late?

FIVE

A crowd of onlookers had gathered around the demolished pharmacy storefront, murmuring and pointing at the man in the dark-blue shirt and wide-brimmed hat. The police were talking to Lyle and Brandon. Ivy looked at the smashed glass windows, which she'd decorated with love year after year at Christmastime. She picked up the broken handmade Welcome sign that she'd hung in the store's window two years ago. What a mess.

When Holly left a few minutes earlier with the car's passenger, the young man tried to follow them. But Brandon stopped him, explaining that unless he was going to the hospital in an ambulance, the law required him to stay at the crash site until the police arrived.

The driver was now facing the wreckage with his head down, fingers pressing into his temples.

Ivy walked closer so no one else could hear. If Holly was sticking her neck out for his passenger, Ivy should try to get as many facts as she could from him. "May I ask you a question?"

"You can ask." The man turned to face her, but it wasn't clear if he intended to answer. His golden-brown eyes looked into hers. She blinked. In another situation she would've found him handsome. Although his wavy auburn hair was cut in the Swartzentruber tradition — below the ears — it didn't look unkempt on him. Still, nice eyes and hair could be deceiving. She needed to get to the bottom of what was really happening here in order to know what to do next.

Was alcohol involved? She'd been taking communion with real wine for a long time, so she knew the smell of alcohol. She just needed to be closer to him.

"I need to know if you've been drinking." She took a quick sniff. He didn't smell of alcohol.

He grimaced. "Drinking? You think I'd drink, especially with her in the car?"

"You were swerving all around and then hit a building. It's a fair question."

"I kept pushing the brake, and it wouldn't work. The man I bought the car from

67

warned me it was a clunker and had been sitting for a while, but I had no idea the brakes would go out."

She remembered his apparent attempt to drive the car into the field only to be blocked by a horse and buggy. His reasoning made sense. "Sorry, I had to ask." She'd overheard the woman say to him *all this to get medicine for me.* "But why not hire a driver to bring you here? I know your community doesn't allow hiring a driver often, but they do in a medical emergency."

The man stared at the still-smoking wreck. "You can't hire a driver if you don't know where or how far you're going."

So they intended to come to the pharmacy for medicine, but afterward they were directionless? That didn't make sense, but he was right that they needed a car of their own in that situation. Maybe her first gut instinct was right. They were most likely in some sort of trouble and trying to run. That was the only thing that made sense.

Ivy crossed her arms. Holly would want to help them, and Ivy needed to at least have their names. "Okay, if you need help — and it seems clear that you do — we need some answers. It's the way things work. So let's start with something simple. I'm Ivy Zook. And your name is? Also, what about the woman you're traveling with? Is she your wife?"

He said nothing.

"That's it?" A shiver of unease ran down Ivy's back. "I mention helping, and you have nothing to say?"

Lyle and Brandon were walking toward them with the police officer.

The officer approached the Swartzentruber man with a device of some type in hand. He also pulled out a notepad and pen. "I'm Officer Jenson with the Raysburg Police. Are you the driver?"

The man faced the officer. "I am. I'm so sorry. I didn't mean for this to happen."

"You're Amish, right?"

The driver nodded. "Swartzentruber Amish."

"Your name?"

"Arlan Keim."

"And your passenger?"

"Magda Keim."

Officer Jenson took notes, and then he looked the man up and down. "Son, it appears that today you're very lucky and very unlucky. Of all the buildings you could have hit, you happened to hit the one belonging to the nicest man in town, Lyle Greene." He pointed a thumb at Lyle, who was standing next to him. "When I arrived, he pulled me aside and asked if there was any way to avoid arresting you for reckless driving. How you answer determines if I'm going to honor his request or not. First question: have you had any alcoholic drink in the last twenty-four hours?"

"No."

The officer held up the small device. "Would you breathe into this for me?"

"Sure."

The officer pressed buttons, and the device beeped. "Put your lips around this, and blow into it hard and steady."

Arlan did as asked. The device beeped again.

"Okay." The officer held the device closer to him, looking at something. "This is good. You have zero percent alcohol. Next question: do you have a driver's license and insurance for that car?"

Arlan dragged a hand down his face. "Ya, I have a license. It's a temporary copy because I just got it Friday. No insurance. I didn't think I'd need it." He reached into his pocket, pulled out a wallet, removed a card that appeared to have his photo on it, and handed it to the officer.

Ivy stared at what little she could see of the license. It wasn't uncommon for Old Order Amish men to get a driver's license once their rumschpringe began. But for a Swartzentruber man to do so was considered worldly and rebellious.

Officer Jenson made a few more notes on his notepad. "So what happened? Start at the beginning."

"I'm sorry. I didn't have a lot of money or time. I bought this car on Saturday for a few hundred dollars, and it seemed fine during the ten-minute drive here. But when I tried to stop in front of the pharmacy to park, the brakes didn't work. I just needed to bring Magda to the pharmacy. She's been unable to eat or keep food down for weeks."

"And your solution was to try to get away from your community without being noticed?" Ivy asked.

"Ya." Arlan shrugged.

The officer scratched his head with the back of his pen. "I'd say the plan to stay out of sight has failed."

Arlan sighed. "If I go to jail, there's no one who can take care of her."

The officer wrote a few more notes. "How old are you?"

"Twenty-two."

The officer squinted as he looked at the driver's license, and then he sighed. "At least you're a legal adult." He closed the notepad and handed the temporary license back to the man. "Look, I have to write a report and it has to include the information that you don't have car insurance, but I'm not going to insist you return home or send you to jail. But doing it this way — Lyle not pressing charges for this destruction — means he won't be able to file the building's damage on his insurance. So you'll need to work out a way to pay him back."

"Ya, of course I will."

"I'm Lyle, and I'm sure we can work this out."

"I'd really appreciate it," Arlan said.

Lyle nodded. "I know a great Amish contractor that I bet will have a crew here in hours." He took a step forward and patted Arlan on the shoulder. "Anyone willing to do all that to get medicine for someone he loves can't be a bad person."

What had Arlan done that had him running like this? To her, his story didn't add up. She needed to talk to Holly. Ivy wasn't sure how much they should help this couple.

Brandon studied the destruction, frowning, but he didn't say anything. Could the pharmacy, which had been on very shaky ground since Lyle's illness eight months ago, take a financial hit like this if the man didn't have any money?

"One last thing." Officer Jenson pointed

at Arlan.

"Yes?"

"You have to promise me *not* to drive again without insurance and a car in good working order. It's never worth the risk. If you or someone you know is in trouble or needs medical help, you call us. We'll get you a ride." He reached in his pocket and handed the young man a card.

"I promise."

Ivy looked at the wrecked storefront again. Promises didn't fix windows, and this town needed Greene's to be open, for Amish and Englisch alike.

Six

Arlan put the last of the trash bags in the dumpster behind the pharmacy. He pulled off his work gloves and walked to the front of the store. He'd been picking up debris and sweeping up glass from the sidewalk for hours. Since he'd swept and washed off the sidewalk, he no longer saw any signs of the shattered glass, and the spaces where the windows had been were now covered by thin sheets of plywood.

He adjusted the baseball cap Ivy had given him. She hadn't been particularly friendly when she handed it and a T-shirt to him, but maybe that was because she'd been tasked to help other employees clean up inside the pharmacy building. After passing him the cap and shirt, she'd told him to push his bangs straight back, tuck what he could of his bowl-cut hair behind his ears, and pull the cap down low so it looked as if he had an Englisch hairstyle. Her next instruction was for him to remove his long-sleeved shirt and wear the T-shirt over his suspenders. As he sweated, the suspenders rubbed against his skin, and he felt as if he was developing blisters. But clearly she understood his need not to look Swartzentruber. How would he explain any of this to Lorraine? He flushed, wondering if she would even speak to him after such a disaster.

The other workers were loading up to leave for the day. He handed the work gloves to one of the Old Order men Lyle had hired. "Denki."

The man tilted his head, curiosity reflecting in his eyes. Embarrassment singed Arlan's cheeks. He'd spoken in Pennsylvania Dutch. Rather than making up an excuse for why he'd used that word, he simply smiled and prayed word didn't get around that an Amish or Swartzentruber man had crashed a car into a store. That would be a surefire way for his parents to learn where Magda and he were. Mamm and Daed already had to be looking for them.

He walked across the street to the Martel Clinic, a trek he'd made several times today, checking on his sister. When he entered this time, the woman at the front desk pressed a button that caused a buzzer to sound, and she motioned for him to go through the door that led to the back. As he walked down the hallway toward Magda's room, he glanced at a clock on the wall. *Six o'clock already?* He'd crashed the car around lunchtime. How was it already this late?

He tapped on the door.

"Kumm rei." His sister still sounded really weak even though they'd been pumping something into her veins for hours.

He went inside Magda's room, and she stirred on the exam bed. She rubbed her eyes as if waking.

"Bischt allrecht?" He'd asked that question every time he'd stepped into this room today. Was she all right?

"Ya." She gave him the same one-word response each time, and then she fell asleep.

He pulled up a chair and sat next to her. The same thoughts kept circling in his brain. He'd had a plan when they left home this morning. They'd get meds for Magda and then keep driving. They could sleep in the car until he found a job that could support them while Magda got well. He'd intended to write his parents tonight and assure them they were safe and would return when the time was right. It hadn't been an ideal plan, but it was doable and one that shouldn't ruin his chance of moving to New York and joining that Swartzen-truber community by this time next year. But now they had nowhere to go, no way for him to search for a job outside this area. They were stuck: Magda was attached to this clinic by an IV bag on a pole. But what would they do when this place closed in three hours? Their sleeping quarters had been towed somewhere.

His face flushed again at the thought of so many people working all day because of him. Because of his mess — a huge one. They were lucky to be alive. Ivy, the Amish girl who was somehow connected to Greene's Pharmacy, had even thought he was drunk and that still nagged at him. But she had also helped.

"Arlan?" Magda stirred and tried to move her arm that was connected to the IV.

"I'm here." He scooted his chair closer to the bed. "You're still at the clinic."

She pushed herself to a sitting position using her free arm. Her face held color, not much, but it was more than it had in weeks.

"You look better." Even though he'd been allowed to see Magda whenever he came into the clinic, no one had told him how she was doing.

"Ya. I feel like I've had some life breathed back into me."

"Gut." It didn't seem right to burden her with unnecessary information about the crash and how he'd need to spend all the money he'd saved and more to cover the cost of repairing the store. Regardless of how generous Lyle was, Arlan would pay every cent it cost to replace that storefront. But he owed more than he could pay at the moment. What on earth were they going to do now?

She fidgeted with the blanket over her. "I have something I need to tell you. You've risked so much to get me help, but if you knew the whole story, you might be dragging me back to Daed and Mamm."

Shame covered her. He could see it as clearly as the prayer Kapp on her head, and he hated it for her. He had good reason to feel shame too, because he was the one who'd introduced her to Rodney. Then Arlan got busy with his own life and didn't keep a watchful eye on his sweet, naive little sister. Maybe Rodney had the most reason to carry shame. Or maybe most of the blame fell on Arlan. "If it's about why you're so very sick, I know."

Her eyes grew wide, and several moments passed before she blinked. "You know?"

"Ya. I overheard Mamm and Daed discussing it. Let's not talk about it." It was a very uncomfortable subject, especially with one's sister. "I knew what I was doing when I left with you."

A tear rolled down one of Magda's cheeks. "But did you consider what trouble this could cause between you and Lorraine?"

"None, I hope. I'll write to her soon, maybe tonight, and explain everything." He wrote to Lorraine a lot. If anything was on his mind, he poured it out in letters, and then he felt better. "It wasn't right for Daed to leave you sick like you've been for weeks. He'll feel different once he calms down. In the meantime we'll get you better. Whatever it takes — days, weeks, a month."

"Nee!" She rattled the pole holding the IV. "That won't be long enough. He'll stick to his plan. I know he will."

Arlan felt the blood drain from his face. What didn't he know? "What *is* his plan, Magda?"

"To hide the pregnancy from everyone, and when the baby is born, they will take my baby as their own."

He sat there, making himself breathe. The idea of taking the baby against Magda's will was mean. God said parents were to be obeyed, but there was nothing in the Bible to justify their parents' plan, was there? "You're sure? Maybe you misunderstood."

"Mamm explained it in detail."

"But . . ." Following that plan would make them hypocrites and liars. He couldn't believe his ears. Lending Magda a hand long enough to get her well and to let Daed rethink his plan was one thing, but staying gone too long would ruin his chance that the New York Swartzentruber bishop would allow Arlan to move there, even though he'd put good money into his brother's farm. Arlan wanted to think through this whole thing right now and come up with a plan. But his mind wouldn't budge from the idea of *hypocrites.*

He saw his Mamm's sweet face in his mind's eye. No wonder she'd been crying for weeks. It wasn't just that Magda was pregnant, although that was enough on its own. It was also that Mamm would need to lie to everyone she knew for the rest of her life, including her own children. He could see how it would be done — with the extra weight Mamm carried all the time and the thick, pleated dress, no one knew when she was pregnant and when she wasn't. "How did they intend to hide your growing belly in the months to come?"

"They would tell others they'd sent me to a cousin's in another state, and I'd stay at the hunting cabin. When my time came,

Mamm would join me."

The hunting cabin was a half-fallen shed an hour from their home. The only source of water was a creek. He couldn't imagine his Daed agreeing to such a plan, let alone devising it. He was a man of honor, wasn't he?

Arlan wouldn't mind his parents' plan so much if Magda agreed with it and the church was aware and okay with it. Mamm and Daed raising Magda's baby as their own made sense for several reasons. Magda could remain near her baby without the stigma of being an unwed mom. She could be courted, fall in love, and marry. Since their youngest brother was only three, it would look to others as if Mamm had simply had another baby. No one would suspect or ask if a newborn in Mamm's arms was Magda's.

"I . . . I'm so sorry." Magda's words broke through Arlan's shock. She looked down as a few more tears fell, blotching the fabric of her dark-green exam gown. "I know you said you didn't want to talk about it, but I'm so sorry."

"Rodney's the father?"

She nodded.

"Are you in love with him?"

"Nee. At first I enjoyed time at the shop

with him. He liked my candles, and for the first time in my life I felt . . . special and appreciated. I've spent my life feeling invisible. And he made me laugh. I . . . I didn't know what was happening at first, but his touch was warm, he was kind to me, and it didn't feel wrong. I felt special, as if I mattered beyond the work I contributed. Later, when my head cleared, the guilt was horrible, and I kept begging God to forgive me. Rodney made it clear I was welcome anytime, and he hoped I'd come back the next day, but I didn't. A few weeks later I realized I was . . . with child. It's not like Mamm ever talked to me as to what caused that."

"Did you tell Rodney about the baby?" He hated the thought, but maybe they could get financial help from Rodney to cover Magda's medicines and the things the baby would need. But if he saw the man again, it'd be hard to resist punching him. Magda hadn't known what was happening, but Rodney knew.

"Ya. I went back to his parents' store and talked to him. He wants nothing to do with it. He told me to find an Englisch doctor that would, in his words, end a pregnancy. He tried to give me money to get it *handled.*" She wiped her cheeks. "Funny how once you see someone for who they really are, you're never the same. What I saw in those moments still haunts me. Rodney never cared about me. But I couldn't agree to Daed's plan either."

"I don't blame you." Arlan shifted in the chair. "Look, wrecking the car set us back, but we're going to figure this out. You're keeping your baby."

"Holly said we could stay at her house when the clinic closes tonight."

"Holly?" Was that the doctor's name? Ivy was the name of the woman who thought he was drunk and gave him this ridiculous hat and T-shirt.

"The Old Order woman who brought me to the clinic. She works at the pharmacy. Doc Jules said that tonight I either needed to stay with Holly so she could check on me or I need to go to the hospital."

Arlan wanted to step outside for a minute and scream at the top of his lungs. Instead he settled for a loud sigh. He didn't like the idea of owing these people more than they already did, which was a lot. But Magda had no insurance for an overnight hospital stay. Added to that, he was unfamiliar with Englisch laws concerning minors. What if the hospital took Magda in as a patient but then had to contact their parents before they could treat her?

"I'm feeling better. Much better. We could just go. Maybe even hitch a ride toward those Englisch farms you said might have jobs for you."

"No. We didn't take these chances to put your health at risk. If the doc says you need to stay at Holly's house, then we stay."

SEVEN

Ivy adjusted the wick on her kerosene lamp, making the flame shine brighter and dispelling some of the darkness. She brushed her hair and twisted it, trying to secure it in a bun that would stay in place all day.

How had their guests slept last night? Ivy, Holly, and Mamm had helped the Swartzentruber couple get settled. Ivy had some reservations about the man but felt sorry for poor Magda. Pregnancy was really walloping her. How young was she, anyway? But, on second thought, it wasn't unusual for Swartzentruber women to marry at eighteen or nineteen. At least last night Magda had a bit of color to her face as she crawled into bed before Ivy shut the door to her and Arlan's bedroom.

A delicious aroma filled the air, and Ivy knew her Mamm was up and cooking, probably wanting to take good care of their guests and hoping to bake something Magda would eat. Holly said that today's goals for Magda were to continue resting and to take in nourishment. Ivy didn't know what might taste good to her, but Holly had said the medicines for nausea were working as well as expected.

Ivy certainly wasn't hungry this time of day. She yawned and rubbed her eyes. If she weren't born into a family of dairy farmers, she would so *not* be a morning person. But the cows wouldn't appreciate waiting until Ivy felt like getting up.

She pinned her prayer Kapp into place. Milking was easier and more fun when Holly helped, which she managed to do about five out of fourteen times per week. Ivy understood. Holly studied until late most nights, and she worked really long hours at the pharmacy. At least the dairy herd was small. Still, it was a lot of taxing work and Ivy hated every minute of it. Although cleaning houses wasn't her dream job, she much preferred doing that with Eva and Dora than anything to do with dairy farming.

Ivy picked up the kerosene lantern, left her bedroom, and headed for the stairs. The hard work wasn't what bothered her. People in all walks of life had to work really hard. What nagged at her all the time was the constant hiding of who she really was. She would put on Amish attire and pin up her hair and work beside her Mamm as if that was who she was. She felt like a hypocrite, like a caged bird — a wild one that someone had caught and shoved into a small space behind bars. Why couldn't Mamm understand that? Why did wanting to leave the Old Ways have to be a betrayal to those Ivy loved?

The guest room door swung open wide, making Ivy jolt slightly. Arlan came to a quick halt inside the doorway. He was dressed. What was he doing up?

"Ah, good morning." She raised her lantern.

The cat seemed to have his tongue as he blinked several times. "Uh, morning."

Ivy looked past him, catching a glimpse of the room. Magda seemed to be asleep, her back facing the door. The side of the bed that should've been Arlan's was undisturbed. Had he taken the time to make it up while Magda was still asleep? Then she saw it: a pallet of blankets and a pillow on the floor. They slept apart? Who were these people that she and Holly had let into their home?

Ivy lowered her eyes and continued walking down the hall toward the stairs. Arlan pulled the door closed and followed her.

She glanced at him over her shoulder. His hands were in his pockets, and he didn't look tired in the least. "Why are you up so early?"

"I'm up to work. You're going out to milk, right?"

"Ya, but you can rest. You and Magda are our guests."

"No. I'm a dairy farmer too. I'm up at this time or earlier every morning. Show me how you milk, and for as long as I'm staying with you, I can give you and your Mamm the mornings off. It's the least I can do."

She didn't want to make him feel bad, because his offer sounded sincere, but how could a Swartzentruber man know how to work the milking machines and be able to follow the guidelines to sell grade A quality milk?

"Um, we'll see."

Doc Jules had said it'd be best if Magda could stay here two weeks. Magda's ultrasound showed that she was near the end of her first trimester, and in two weeks she would be in the second trimester. Most women started feeling a lot better at that point.

When she walked into the kitchen, Mamm

was at the sink, rinsing fresh fruit.

"Morning, Mamm. Our guest said he was going to help me milk." She glanced at Arlan. Did she want his help? He'd yet to tell them what was really going on and why he and his wife were hiding from their own people.

Mamm dusted some flour off her apron. "Good morning. It's Arlan, right?"

Arlan nodded.

"Maybe you caught my name last night when I said it, but I'm Betty Zook."

"Denki for your hospitality, Betty."

Mamm smiled and nodded, but she didn't look at them. Was she avoiding making eye contact with Ivy?

"Arlan, if you could take my place in the milking parlor this morning, I'll stay in and finish breakfast." Mamm wiped her hands on a dish towel, never glancing in Ivy's direction.

How on earth could Ivy move into her new apartment without completely breaking her relationship with Mamm? There had to be a way, didn't there? They hadn't spoken more than a few words to each other since Ivy divulged her plans four days ago. In Ivy's estimation there was no cause for friction. She was her own person, and wanting to be someone different than what her

Mamm and the community expected of her wasn't intended to insult or harm Mamm.

"Ya, I'd be grateful to step in and help the farmhands in your stead," Arlan said.

Was Mamm avoiding being in the same room with her?

"Coming." Holly's voice preceded her as she hurried down the stairs. "Sorry. I studied until nearly one, and then I overslept." She rushed into the kitchen, still in her nightgown and housecoat. "I'm desperate for coffee first, though." She caught a glimpse of Arlan and gasped. *"Ach."*

"Your morning has just taken a turn for the better," Ivy said. "Arlan is helping. Get some sleep before you have to go to work."

Holly breathed a sigh of relief. "Bless you." She smiled at Arlan and turned to Ivy. "You sure?"

Her sister deserved to sleep. "Go, sleepyhead."

"You're the best sis ever." Holly yawned and left the room much slower than she'd entered it.

Ivy looked at Mamm. "Remind her of that the next time I make her mad."

"Ya?" Mamm said. "When will that be, October?"

Mamm's jab was uncharacteristic. Ivy stifled a sigh and walked outside with the lantern in hand. The night sky was a deep purple as the sun grew closer to peeping over the horizon. The brightest of stars were still visible. A whip-poor-will sang and crickets chirped. If time allowed, she'd love to take a cup of coffee to her and Mamm's favorite sitting spot and welcome each new day. Being up this early could be a blessing. Milking cows . . . not so much.

She went to the side of the barn, and Arlan followed close behind.

Before she could set the lantern on the ground, he took it from her and held it up, studying her. "Are no menfolk coming to help?"

His question made her heart sting. "No."

"But . . ."

"My Daed died eleven years ago this October, and my brother, Red, lives and works in Rocks Mill." Her family was odd compared to most Amish. They were the smallest family she knew of, and three women were breadwinners and tended the farm. "There's no money to hire dairy hands, but on the upside we only have ten cows, and of those there are eight to milk. We hire men to sow and harvest the hayfields. Other than that the women run the farm. Can we get to work now?"

"Ya."

She pointed. "We have three generators. The one used for cooling the milk tanks stays running all the time, and it has a backup, because without refrigerated milk tanks, we lose our ability to sell it as grade A. We sell to Troyer Yogurt and Cheese, a booming business that makes specialty items. The milk must be grade A because they advertise it as such." She flipped the On button of the smallest generator. "This one only runs during milking times." She pulled the choke. "It powers the milkers and pumps the milk into the milk tank." She pulled the starter handle, yanking the cord toward her, and the generator came to life.

Then they walked into the barn. It was weird being in this familiar place with a stranger, especially a man.

"Okay" — she held up a set of milkers — "this is how things work, and every step is important, either for the cows' health or the quality of milk." She gave him a rundown of the milking process. He listened in silence, not asking so much as one question. Should she insist he go back inside?

She gestured at the row of milkers connected to the piping that led to the milk tank. "Have you ever used milking machines before?"

"Many times. The machines aren't so

hard. Way easier than doing it by hand."

Huh. Which was the bigger surprise from this Swartzentruber — pulling out a driver's license at the wreck yesterday or having used generator-powered milking machinery?

"Well, gut. Let's get started. You can begin by climbing into the haymow and tossing down a few bales of straw. I'll get a pitchfork and start spreading it into the stalls before the cows come in." Maybe she didn't need to tell him that part, but dairy barns were similar to women's kitchens — each one was run differently, based on equipment and personal preferences. "Then toss down bales of hay for feeding."

He moved fast, and soon the first four cows were in their milking stalls.

They went through the usual process — cleaning the teats, drying them, and connecting the milkers. Despite how quickly he moved, he was skilled at calming the cows, and he followed her instructions carefully.

As they began working with the second set of cows, Arlan cleared his throat. "I just want to say thank you."

She was on a milking stool, attaching a set of milkers. She turned to look at him over her shoulder. "Ya." She couldn't make herself tell him he was welcome. The words wouldn't form. "You needed help, and that's my family's thing — not ignoring people in need."

"I'm glad." He gave her a half smile before turning back to the cow.

She grabbed the milking stool and tub that held the cleaners and drying cloths. "For someone who's been raised Swartzentruber Amish, you're quite comfortable with this kind of milking system."

"Ah, that." He patted the cow he'd just finished attaching to the milkers and stood. "There were years when my older brother and Daed were all the hands our farm needed, so I brought in money by working for various Englisch and Old Order farms."

Why hadn't he told her that *before* she explained how everything worked?

"So why'd you and your wife leave?" Ivy should mind her own business, but she just couldn't.

He didn't respond.

Ivy moved to the next cow. "It seems odd that you slept on the floor."

"Are all Old Order Amish women as intrusive as you?"

"Definitely not." She rubbed the side of Daisy Mae's udder. "Good girl," she cooed. "But maybe they should be."

Were Arlan and Magda even husband and wife? Once the milkers were attached, she stood so she could see Arlan. "Are you . . . in love with her?"

"No, ugh!" He shuddered and made a face like he'd smelled spoiled milk before he regained his composure.

Suddenly the pieces clicked together. They were related, maybe brother and sister. Thinking about it, she realized the two looked a bit alike. They had the same brown-and-gold eyes. "And so she's your . . ."

He sighed. "My sister."

Ivy had no idea if she liked what she'd just learned. It was easier to think of them as husband and wife than to realize Magda was pregnant and on the run from someone.

Blue Bonnet mooed loudly, a clear indication she wasn't relaxed or comfortable.

He went to her and rubbed her sides. "I'm sorry for not telling you the truth. But the less everyone knows, the less chance it can get back to our parents. There are only a few Swartzentruber families left in this area."

They were running from their parents? A shiver ran through Ivy. Then Dora and Eva came to mind. "I know. I'm a friend with two Swartzentruber girls, ones I can't afford to offend." If Mamm stayed upset with Ivy, Mamm would need someone to help her clean houses. "If I were caught hiding you or Magda, it could cause my family to lose that relationship."

He crouched and removed the milkers from Blue Bonnet.

"And this?" Ivy pointed at his lower face.

"I don't know." He touched his chin whiskers. "It made sense a few days ago to let it grow out as if I was a married man, just in case we still looked Amish when we checked into a hotel or something. Most Englisch seem to know that when a couple is married, the man has a beard."

"You didn't think the car would give you away?"

"Beachy Amish drive cars, and I don't figure most Englisch can tell one sect of Amish from another." He moved to the last cow.

That seemed quite true.

"Look." Ivy passed him the milking stool. "You don't have to worry about me or anyone else in my family passing information about you and Magda to other people. But maybe you're going at this all wrong."

He put the milkers back on the cow and stood, facing Ivy. "You might think you know a lot about our order, but until you've lived it, I doubt you could understand. Leaving home is all we can do for now. If this gets back to our parents, they'll come for Magda and it will break her." He grimaced, and she saw pain in the lines on his face. "And I can't allow that."

Then why not just leave your order? "No one wants that. No one."

"Denki." His shoulders seemed to relax. "I'm glad to hear it. Really glad."

"You don't need to continue sleeping on the floor in the same room as your sister. There's a mattress in the back bedroom upstairs. We currently use that space for storage, so it'll take some organizing."

"I saw that you have a room above the carriage house. Could I use that?"

"Sure." It didn't have any running water, but apparently that was within his comfort zone.

"I appreciate it." He sounded relieved. "Nothing has worked out like I thought. And your home is so different — with the running water and the gas-powered appliances." He grabbed a pitchfork and began mucking an empty stall. "I hardly slept last night for feeling as if I was in a fancy Englischer home."

"You say that as if it's sinful."

He paused and studied her. Did he disapprove of her? Not that she cared. It was just annoying.

He removed the stool and left the stall. "A lot of work needs to be done around here." He hung the stool on a peg on the wall and grabbed the pitchfork. "I can milk and mend what's broken and —"

"Sure. Fine. I could stand two weeks of not needing to milk cows, muck stalls, or climb into that haymow." She set the rags and cleaners in their holder on the barn wall. "Actually if I never milked another cow, it would be too soon — with or without all possible modern conveniences."

He stared at her again. "But your life here is so easy . . . and worldly."

Worldly? She'd stick to the topic of *easy* for now. "Easy? You think because we have indoor plumbing and generators to help out in our barn that our life is easy?"

His eyes flickered with hardness before he set aside the pitchfork and removed the milkers from Cutie Pie, but he said nothing. He didn't have to.

Ivy couldn't budge. "You think I'm a horrible sinner because the Old Order are okay with more modernization than the Swartzentrubers are, but I've got news for you. I think entirely too many of our Old Ways are unnecessary. So judge that."

He stood there, early morning light now pouring through the dirty windows and various knotholes and between the boards that made up the wall of the barn. Particles of dust that always hung in the air were easily visible now, and it reminded her of how much unseen murkiness and haze were between any two people.

Still, he could finish by himself. Ivy strode out of the barn.

EIGHT

Holding a wide paintbrush, Holly gazed at the beautiful white farmhouse in the distance that stood tall and welcoming, despite needing a good coat of paint. That would have to be a future painting project. But today she and Josh were painting the *Daadi Haus,* a home that Josh's Mamm and Daed would move into right before Holly and Josh's wedding.

Holly clutched her paintbrush and dipped it into the tray of white paint. She could hardly wait to live on this chicken farm as Josh's wife. Some of his chickens were near them in the yard, milling about. The rolling hills were lush with the verdant green of summer. She loved this place. A moment later thoughts of her sister pushed in. Something was weighing on Ivy, something she was keeping from Holly. That alone said a ton. And there was tension between her and Mamm, but why?

"Hey, Holly, think fast." Josh flicked paint her way.

Holly laughed as she dodged the splatter of white paint. "Josh Smucker, don't you dare! You know that I'm going to work after this. Jules will be here any minute."

He grinned. "I saw you looking at our future home." He slapped the brush against the clapboard house.

She chuckled and pressed the brush against the house. "I was admiring it *while* painting on this small home for your folks."

They were finishing a section of outside wall. Since they weren't hiring someone to do the painting and they both worked, they only did small sections at a time. His Mamm seemed pleased with the adorable cottage so far and was even more excited about the wedding. The late-morning sun was getting hotter, so it was probably good that they'd have to pause this project soon. But thanks to Arlan's help on the dairy farm the last ten days, Holly was more free to be here with Josh, getting this homestead ready for when they would begin their life together.

She swiped the brush horizontally along the clapboard. "Ivy's on my mind again."

"Ya, I know. I can see it in those gorgeous eyes of yours, but she'll confide in you before long."

"I hope so." Holly moved the paintbrush up one board.

"You could threaten to paint her clothes with your handprints."

Holly's cheeks burned. "Joshua Smucker, you shush."

He dipped his brush back into his paint tray and wiped off the excess on the sides. "You know I'll have to walk by my parents when I go back in the house, and it'll look like you were trying to grab —"

"Hey," — Holly put both hands up in the air, with one still holding her brush — "it was a total accident! I tripped, touched the painted wall on my way down, and then grabbed the closest thing so I didn't fall into the paint bucket. It just so happened to be you. Tell him, Becky. You were there."

The yellow Buff Orpington chicken turned her head toward Holly and then went back to foraging the area for bugs.

"Sure, sure." Josh winked.

She still felt butterflies in her stomach when she looked at him, even though he was messy, sweaty, and covered in paint. In about six months they'd be husband and wife. Over-the-moon elation and uncertainty mixed together like white and black paint.

As excited as they both were, they weren't home free yet. Amish women didn't work outside the home after marriage, at least not until the youngest child was in school. Produce stands were allowed. Sometimes women were allowed to clean a person's home or to have a cottage industry that included baking, sewing, or handmade crafts. But an Amish woman couldn't have a career with set hours that kept her away from home. It was a hard-and-fast rule she'd known since she was small. But she'd worked so hard to become a bridge that linked modern medicine to the area's Amish communities, first by working as a pharmacy tech at Greene's and then one day, God willing, by being an LPN. Holly was so thankful that her bishop valued her work and, after a heartfelt conversation, was happy to approve of her marriage to Josh. With the living arrangements on the Smucker family chicken farm, a successful business Josh had worked hard to build since he was a teen, someone would always be nearby to help with any future children, even with Holly continuing to work. But she'd never met Josh's bishop. Word had it that Bishop Stephan was a stickler for tradition.

Josh swiped another broad brushstroke on

the wall. "You have that lost-in-thought look again. What's on your mind? Plotting your next paint crime?"

Holly shook off the worries like shedding a heavy coat and grinned. "You know it."

"Aha, so you admit it now."

She narrowed her eyes, but before she could come up with a good retort, tires crunched on the gravel driveway. Jules was here.

She set her paintbrush next to the rest of the supplies and pulled off her painting apron. She'd be back tomorrow to help again. "Next time, Smucker."

"Next time I better wear a head-to-toe cover-up. Got it." He smiled at her. "Have a great day at work, Holly. Love you. I know you're worried about getting everything handled before the wedding, but we have this."

"Love you too." They'd talked about his bishop numerous times, and Josh was trying to ease the man into the twenty-first century concerning Holly's job, but it was no easy feat to get an Amish bishop to think outside the Old Ways. Josh felt hopeful about it, and he had time to continue talking to his bishop since it was nearly half of a year until December.

She walked to the driveway and hopped

into Julie's car. "Thanks for the ride."

Julie adjusted the rearview mirror. "It's no trouble at all, especially with our schedules lining up today. How's Magda feeling?"

"Good. But she's still sick to her stomach at times, even with the nausea meds."

"I checked on her last week, but I'd like to do so again before they leave the area." Jules picked up her speed.

Holly used a fingernail to scrape at some dried paint on her forearm. "Sure. Anytime that works for you. They don't leave the farm right now."

It seemed that everyone on the Zook farm except her had a secret. Arlan and Magda didn't want their parents to discover where they were staying. Mamm was unhappy with Ivy for reasons she didn't want to talk about. But what weighed on Holly was Ivy's secret.

What was going on in her little sister's life that was so bad she wasn't talking to Holly about it?

With a rope tied around his waist and the far end of it anchored to a rafter inside the barn, Arlan used every muscle in his body as he maneuvered across the roof to put a new sheet of tin into place. Sweat poured as the bright July sun bore down. It was still morning, maybe eleven, but he felt as if he was standing in an oven.

In his two weeks of being here, he'd found plenty of wood, tin, and nails in the carriage house to make repairs. The only thing this farm lacked was manpower. He removed his work gloves and shoved them into his tool belt before kneeling and hammering the metal into place. When it was finally secured, he put the tools in his belt and used the rope to climb to a hole he had made in the roof, a small area he'd have to seal and waterproof when the job was complete. He shimmied through the hole and landed on his feet in the hayloft. After removing the rope, he climbed down the haymow's ladder. The repairs to the roof were almost finished. He needed only one more sheet of tin.

He stepped out of the dairy barn, wishing he could go to his favorite stream to cool off. The shower inside the house did the job. He got plenty clean. But in other ways it made him feel dirtier. Did that make him a hypocrite? It wasn't as if he kept all the Swartzentruber rules — either here or at home. Since moving into the room above the carriage house, he'd spent time each evening reading one of the fiction books he'd brought with him. He also wrote to

Lorraine in the evenings, although he'd yet to send a letter. Even so, writing made him feel connected to his dreams.

While walking toward the carriage house to get the last needed piece of tin, he spotted Magda in the vegetable garden to the left of the house. She was picking fist-sized tomatoes and placing them in a basket. His heart warmed. She was getting better. They could do this. But it was time to talk to Magda about leaving soon.

"Hallo," Magda called, smiling. Then she bent down and pulled a weed.

He returned her wave and headed that way. When he and Magda left here, hopefully in the next day or two, nothing would leak, and no one would be at risk of a rung breaking or being gouged by a rusted, broken nail. He felt good that he was leaving this place in better condition than when he'd arrived. He'd even fixed the steps to the room above the carriage house. That space was now suitable for the Zooks to rent out, as long as the person was like him and didn't mind living without plumbing. It was an easy walk to the house, and Betty could provide meals for the hired help.

Once beside his sister, he crouched and pulled several weeds and tossed them on the pile Magda had started. "Isn't it a little

hot for you to be working in the garden?"
Did Betty know she was out here weeding?
Even in the borrowed Old Order clothes,
which had fewer layers and were made of
lighter material, the heat had to be hard on
a pregnant woman.

"Ha. This is light duty compared to what
I'd be doing at home, and you know it."
She wiped her forehead with her sleeve.

He knew that for sure, but she'd almost
landed in the hospital just two weeks ago.
He felt as if he'd repaid the debt to Betty,
Ivy, and Holly, but it would be harder to
pay Lyle for all the damages to the pharmacy. The sooner he could find a job, the
sooner he could start sending funds to
Greene's to chip away at his debt for both
the crash and Magda's medicines. However,
he wasn't sure farmers were hiring now like
they were ten years ago. There was a lot of
dormant farmland around these parts, both
where he lived and here. Would that be true
farther north also? Even if it was, how was
he going to earn his parents' good graces
once he returned home? Would the New
York Swartzentrubers understand his actions? Would Lorraine?

He tried not to dwell on these questions.
Surely God would give him insight when
the time came. Whatever he needed to do

later to repent, he knew for sure that his best chance of smoothing things over would be not staying here one day longer than was medically necessary. The two sects were outwardly polite, but the Swartzentrubers — or at least his small community — harbored prejudices against the Old Order. He struggled with the more lenient ways himself, although their love and kindness to him and his sister seemed very biblical.

His sister pointed to the large basket of shiny tomatoes that was sitting on the ground. "When I fill this basket, Betty and I are going to make some sauce and then can it. Later we're going to try a new soap recipe. After a week of resting, I couldn't take it anymore, so last week I made milk-and-honey soaps. Did you know that she took them to a farmer's market yesterday? She sold all twelve bars. I made forty-eight dollars!"

"Magda . . ." He hated to deflate her excitement, but he had to. "You know it's time for us to leave, right?"

Her smile fell. "I . . . I'm not ready, and they like us here. I know Betty does."

Betty did seem to enjoy their presence. She was busy with cleaning houses, and she'd voiced time and again how nice it was not to need to milk the cows too. It was a bit odd that Betty talked to Arlan earlier today about her possibly needing to increase the herd, but the conversation seemed unrelated to Magda and Arlan staying. Betty seemed to simply need information about a topic Arlan was familiar with.

"Magda, we need to go and soon. Look at you. You're well enough to make soaps and weed the garden. We can get enough anti-nausea tablets from the pharmacy to get you through any more bouts of sickness. This isn't our home."

Magda went from crouching to sitting. "I know you're still planning to work for Englisch farmers up north, but hear me out. Before we arrived here, a widow and her two daughters held this farm together. Betty wants us here. She already told me that we could stay longer. She said we could stay all the way until December when the baby is born. Longer, even."

That wasn't at all the impression Arlan had from Ivy, not that he'd spoken with her much since their conversation in the barn the first morning he and Magda were here. She cleaned homes with her Mamm and had some sort of side business.

"You're not thinking this through."

"But Betty's thrilled at all you've been —"

"I know." He really didn't want to hear

any more. "And I'm glad she doesn't think we've overstayed our welcome. I also know it feels like we're in a new land, but we're only eight miles from home. A forty-five-minute buggy ride or ten-minute car ride isn't far enough to keep our whereabouts quiet for much longer. Word is going to spread, and someone from home will find us."

She shook her head. "Nee. Betty told her bishop that we're here. He said that he would visit when time allows and that he welcomes Swartzentruber Amish and that no one will turn us in. You know how the Amish are, Swartzentruber or Old Older. When we agree to keep a thing quiet in our home or community, it stays quiet. The Zooks' bishop said we can even go to church next Sunday."

How could she think that getting comfortable with the Old Order ways was good for them?

He pulled several more weeds. "We're too close. Besides that, what are you thinking? You sound as if you're getting used to this life."

She plucked a few blades of grass from the ground. "Is that such a bad thing?"

Was he now the parent who had to correct her? "Our parents were wrong to treat you as they did, but they are our family, and I believe in our way of life. Don't fall for this cushy way of living, Magda."

"My entire life I've hauled water from our hand pump in the yard — all day, every day. Maybe having indoor water isn't a temptation. Maybe it's an invitation to relax and enjoy life."

Was it her nature to be easily pulled away from their ways? "You know why we don't have that at home. In Jesus's day they had a community well. Why is that not good enough for us? How can we follow Him if we can't even bear dealing with something so simple?"

"But they didn't have hand pumps outside their houses either, and we do. Did Jesus ever say, 'Don't have running water in your house'?"

He stood and looked at the Zooks' house. Why was he arguing with his seventeen-year-old sister? She'd obviously been spending too much time with Betty — and maybe Ivy. These people weren't a good influence.

Magda got up, walked over to Arlan, and looked him in the eye. "I appreciate everything you've done, everything you've sacrificed to get me here and feeling better. I know it's not been easy for you. But I'm staying."

He couldn't believe his ears. "Just like that? Decision made? You don't care that if you're caught, you'll be hauled back home?"

"I won't be caught, and if I get sick again, I have Doc Jules to give me fluids and medicine. She's working with a midwife to make sure my baby is healthy. I think I'm starting to believe that both of us" — she rested a hand on her belly — "will make it through this alive. But I understand if you need to go home."

Everything in him disagreed with her assessment of the Old Order ways, but he couldn't force her to leave, and he wasn't leaving without her. "The only reason I'm here is because of you. If I went home without you, Daed and Mamm would demand to know where you are. I wouldn't tell them, but I'd be in worse trouble than if I just stay gone." If he returned but didn't repent and confess where Magda was, Lorraine's bishop would never allow him to join the New York community.

"Denki."

"I don't want to be thanked. Do you understand how our people will feel about us staying in an Old Order Amish home? We can explain the last two weeks. You had serious medical needs, and I worked the farm to help pay for the Zooks' kindness.

We can't explain staying any longer than two weeks. We need to leave."

She pursed her lips and nodded. "I'm sure Mamm and Daed have checked with the New York community to see if we turned up there. Have you told Lorraine where we are? She'll be worried."

His sister was probably feeling guilty for the trouble his absence from their community could cause with Lorraine, her family, and the church leaders.

"I've written a lot, but I haven't sent a letter yet." He used both hands to pick up the mound of pulled weeds. It was odd how good it felt simply to write even if he didn't mail the letter. He hadn't expected that. "But I didn't mention the baby."

Magda frowned. "Then what was there to say?"

"My thoughts and feelings about you being so sick and us leaving, about me buying a car and what it felt like to leave. Do you mind if I tell her about . . . the baby?"

"It's fine. I've repented of my sin, and I'll own up to my mistake to whoever I need to, but I'm raising this child. You're free to tell her all of that. Just don't give her this address, okay?"

He'd given up everything to help his sister, and now she refused to leave with him? "I will tell her, and she's sure to feel obligated to share that with her bishop. So I suggest you plan on saying your goodbyes to the Zook family, and we leave in two days." He had specific tasks he wanted to complete before they left. It seemed the right thing to do, and it would be very helpful to Betty and Ivy if he finished them.

"And go where?" Magda dusted her hands together. "And how will we get there?"

"You get yourself ready. God will provide the answers soon enough."

His sister stared at him. "You're being unreasonable."

"Me?" Was that true?

"You sound like Daed."

His shoulders slumped. He never wanted to sound like their Daed. "Magda, we're gambling with both of our futures if we stay here. Mine because I'll be in so much more trouble for continuing to stay at an Amish home. And you're at risk because you're a minor. If someone shows up, you could be forced to return home."

"This is our safest place to be, Arlan. We're welcome. Betty said that she and her daughters would appreciate our staying. Your work is valued. If I need medical assistance, it's available. We never would've dreamed God would open such a place to us. It and the Zooks are a gift."

He sat on the grass, mulling over his sister's words. Why didn't he just leave Magda here and go? She was safe. He could return home and refuse to say where she was until she turned eighteen, which would happen in three months. He didn't know the answer to his question, but his reasons for not leaving seemed to run deeper than its causing more trouble for him to return and yet not inform them where Magda was. He'd helped Magda run away, and he couldn't imagine leaving her behind.

Magda glanced at him. "If you send a letter to Lorraine, even without including the address, she'll know what area we're in by the postmark on the letter. That could be enough of a clue for us to be found. Doc Jules asked us to stay two weeks at a bare minimum. Let's be safe in every possible way and stay longer."

Maybe she was right. He could do some bigger projects on the farm if he had more time, and he certainly didn't want to leave with Magda if she might relapse. "Two more weeks, Magda. Just two. Then we have to go somewhere else so I can earn money to put toward paying Mr. Greene back for the storefront window."

"You gave him all we had. How much

more do you owe?"

"I'm unsure. He doesn't want to say the amount outright, but I imagine it's a few thousand dollars."

Magda nodded. "Maybe you could find a way to earn money from here. I'll make more soaps, and you can have every penny of the money I earn."

He didn't want her money. He wanted her cooperation in leaving.

Magda started to say something, but the sound of a car pulling up caught their attention. His heart raced. Had their parents found them?

Ivy got out of the vehicle. She noticed him and gave a little wave. The muscles across his shoulders relaxed, and he returned the wave.

He had no desire to be unyielding like his Daed, but was he compromising too much by staying here? Worse, was he letting himself be led around by a house full of women?

NINE

Ivy closed the door of Tegan's small sedan, watching Arlan and Magda in the side yard next to the garden. At least Magda had on some of Ivy's clothes so she didn't attract the attention of those who pulled up their long driveway. Arlan was the sore thumb sticking out because of his long hair. She rolled her eyes. Juvenile, yes, but no one saw her response. He was just standing out in the open.

Tegan opened her car door, stepped out, and cupped her hand over her eyes to block the sun. "Who's that?"

"He's the guy that's staying with my family and sleeping in the carriage house. And the woman is his sister."

"Oh, the one who's been milking the cows for you." Tegan grinned at Ivy across the top of the car. "He's not bad looking. But it's hard to tell with that hat."

Tegan didn't know he was a Swartzentruber, so Ivy had no need to tell her to keep his presence a secret.

Ivy leaned an elbow on the top of the car. "It wouldn't matter if he was the most handsome man in the state. Trust me." It was time for him and Magda to leave any day now. That was yet another uncomfortable subject to bring up with Mamm. She seemed to be encouraging them to stay. "He believes his thinking is on target and everybody else is missing the target by miles."

"Yeah, you're right. It wouldn't matter how good looking he is. On a better note, you have good news for your mom."

"I do." But Ivy's insides clenched. "Still, my leaving is a sore topic, whether we're talking October or January." Ivy had felt forced into a hard conversation this morning with her future landlord. Clara had been reluctant, but she had finally agreed to Ivy's compromise. Mamm should be relieved. "Regardless of how Mamm feels, we continue booking parties and making plans for our future, Tegan."

Tegan pointed at her. "That's my future roommate." She opened her car door. "See you soon."

"Ya. Okay."

Tegan started her car and drove down the long gravel driveway. Ivy drew a deep

119

breath. *I come bearing good news, Mamm.* Ivy's plan for moving out had become equivalent to a clothesline running through the kitchen, one she and Mamm had bumped into daily for the past couple of weeks. No more avoiding the subject.

She went through the screen door and into the house. "Mamm?"

"I'm here, in the kitchen."

She entered the room to see Mamm sterilizing glass mason jars in a pot of boiling water, lifting them out with tongs, and placing them on clean towels. How many times over the years had Ivy canned delicious homegrown vegetables and fruits with Mamm? Could they ever go back to that kind of closeness — the kind that caused them to enjoy each other's company whether milking cows, cleaning Englisch homes, or planting and harvesting their garden? Or would Ivy leaving the Amish ruin all that? She'd never joined the church, so she'd be allowed some leeway to visit. But would Mamm permit her to? If she allowed it, would she lower her guard and give up her anger with Ivy? Ivy couldn't imagine not being able to talk with Mamm.

There were slices of freshly baked bread laid out on a plate, leftover ham and turkey cut into pieces, and various condiments sitting on the table. Apparently sandwiches were on the menu for lunch.

Ivy spotted two quilted trivets on the kitchen counter that she and Mamm had made together probably five years ago. "I remember these." They'd found the uniquely patterned aqua, pink, orange, purple, and green fabrics on sale at a market. There wasn't enough of each fabric to make a quilt, so they'd made two trivets that looked like miniature quilts, each with a star pattern at the center.

Mamm looked up and gave her a hint of a smile. "That was a good day." She placed the last jar on the towel and turned off the stove.

Ivy touched the trivets' soft fabric. "We need to talk about my plans. I spoke with Tegan and Clara this morning, and I'm going to wait to move out until after the first of the year as you asked. It's going to be tough, but I'll pay my portion of the rent from October to January while still living here. That gives time for Holly's wedding and for all of us to enjoy Christmas together."

"I appreciate the effort. I do."

"But?"

"I got a call earlier today, and the people at Troyer Yogurt and Cheese plan to expand their business. They made it clear they want to keep getting milk from us, but for numerous reasons they must get all their milk from the same place, which means we either take on more cows or lose the contract with them." Mamm reached into a cabinet beside the stove, pulled out a second large pot, and placed it on the burner.

"Mamm, that just confirms it's time to sell the cows we have and shut down the milking parlor. You can't do all the work by yourself with what we have now, so you can't take on more cows."

Mamm stared into the pot. "You could stay." She lifted her eyes to Ivy. "I need you."

A sewing needle jabbed Ivy's heart. "I know you don't want to give up the dairy farm. It's a part of who you and Daed were, and letting it go feels as if you're letting go of all those dreams and all that love you and Daed shared. But I *am* leaving. I'm sorry it'll dismantle so many of your plans, and I'm sorry you'll be caught in the middle between the church and me. I really am. My leaving has nothing to do with how much I love and respect you, but I am leaving."

"You don't get it, do you? This farm *is* who you are. It's in your blood. It was a part of your Daed when he was a boy. It's in almost every memory you have since you were born."

Ivy eased forward. "You are those things to me, Mamm, not this farm." Ivy leaned in, trying to catch her Mamm's eye. "Holly is marrying and moving to another district. Red's not here. Your two Swartzentruber guests won't be here much longer. Why don't we use this time while I'm still at home to get the farm ready to sell?"

"Kumm, Ivy." Mamm walked out of the kitchen and into the living room. Ivy followed. *What is she doing?*

They walked through the living room and into the craft room in the back of the house — Ivy's favorite room. In the mornings sunlight poured through the tall windows. On the walls without windows, Daed had built floor-to-ceiling shelves to hold supplies, and he had installed ample wood counters that folded up for more space. Ivy touched the soft recliner where so many times Daed had sat and chatted with her and Mamm while they worked on crafts together. The room even had a roller propane tank that powered a lamp and often other craft items, such as candle molds and hot glue guns.

Mamm picked up a faceless doll from one of the shelves. Oh, how Ivy had enjoyed making this, her first big sewing project, when she was only seven. Mamm handed it to Ivy. "This is who we've always been. This is who we can continue being. You love making people happy, but throwing well-planned parties isn't the only fulfilling way to touch people's lives with joy. You already decorate Greene's Pharmacy, why not make decorating stores in downtown your business for every holiday? You can enjoy music in Englisch houses while you clean and continue leading the Christmas caroling every year. You could travel to various towns during their arts and crafts shows and get new ideas that are just as exciting as any party-planning jobs. Put your creative talents to good use right here. You can't have everything, but with some effort, I think you could find something even better."

Mamm had thought this through, and her points sounded valid. Ivy wished she could accept them. "Mamm, if I were to stay Amish, I'd still have all the rules of the *Ordnung* imposed on me, constantly directing my life. What I wear, how I travel, how I build my business — everything is ruled by the Ordnung. And when everyone moves on from this farm, and that'll be soon, I'll be back to living your life, not mine."

Mamm's eyes swam with unshed tears.

"Okay." She wiped her eyes and walked out of the craft room.

Ivy set the little doll back on her shelf and followed. "Mamm, don't walk off. Where are you going?"

Without answering Mamm went to the front of the house, stepped onto the porch, and rang the dinner bell.

"We're still talking."

"I think you've said it all, Ivy, and it's lunchtime. After that Magda and I are making tomato sauce and canning it." Mamm straightened one of the rocking chairs.

A moment later Arlan and Magda came into view and soon were on the front porch.

"Arlan, tell Ivy what you told me about the cows this morning."

Was now really the time to talk about cows?

Arlan looked from Ivy to her Mamm, seeming leery of what he'd walked into. "Oh, um, I was just saying that the reason you're having so much trouble making money selling your milk is you don't have enough cows to support the overhead."

More cows was not the direction Mamm needed to go. "So you got a call from Troyer Yogurt and Cheese, and then Arlan explained what a great idea it was to increase the herd? Is that it?"

Mamm fidgeted with the top rail of the rocker. "You know that we loaned out our cows after Ezra died, asking various relatives to hold on to some of the herd. They've tended to them and profited from it. At the time I couldn't make myself sell them. The idea made me sick, as if I were selling your Daed's dreams or a part of his soul. But I talk to those relatives all the time, and they'd be willing to give us a cow or two whenever I'm ready. Not those same cows, of course. I doubt they're still alive. But the family would be generous, if for no other reason than I'm a widow trying to make ends meet."

Or you could sell our cows to them and make good money.

Ivy refused to look at Arlan for fear she'd be overcome by emotion and shove him off the porch. Mamm opened the screen door and held it. Magda lowered her head, looking uncomfortable, but she went inside.

Ivy bit her tongue, aching to speak her mind. She'd presented Mamm with a perfectly good compromise — that she would wait until January to leave — but that didn't seem to matter one ounce. "Since our conversation is done, I'll end with the information that I'll stay until January for Holly's sake. But that's it, Mamm."

Mamm's eyes narrowed, but she said nothing as she went inside after Magda.

Ivy turned to Arlan. "Apparently you have Mamm's ear, so I need you to talk realistically to her about this farm. She's a fifty-three-year-old widow who will have an empty nest in six months. There's no way it's a good idea for her to increase the herd."

"She asked me direct questions, and I answered her, Ivy. That's all."

"But she's clearly listening to you, and she needs to hear the truth."

"Doesn't she, of all people, know what the workload will be if she increases the herd?"

"She's blinded right now, hoping for a miracle. Someone should look out for this widow and tell her the truth of the matter. Okay?"

His brows furrowed, and he looked unsure. "I'll think about it."

He'll think about it? Anger pounded Ivy as she walked into the house.

TEN

Evening light shone through the new plate-glass windows of the pharmacy as the last few customers of the day continued to shop. Holly smiled at the blond-and-gray-haired Old Order woman standing at the pharmacy counter. "Rosanna, I'm so glad you came in today to pick up your meds. I was getting worried you would run out."

"Truth be told, I wasn't sure you were open, what with the accident and all."

Holly's smile wavered at the thought, and she tried to shore it up. Greene's had been closed only two days, and even now, three weeks later, those couple of days were having long-reaching effects on their business. "Nope, we're good as new."

"I can see that." Rosanna looked over her shoulder. Ivy was in the display section of the new windows, hanging shiny tinsel and Christmas lights.

What a relief to have the front of the

pharmacy whole again! It'd taken a while to make and ship the new plate glass in the exact size they needed. Before the glass was installed, Greene's had temporarily used a side entrance for both employees and customers, and the store's business had been obviously slower without the easy-to-access front door. Yesterday Ivy came up with the idea to put out some of the Christmas decorations for a few days — or weeks — to attract attention to the fact that Greene's pharmacy had new windows and a fully repaired front entrance. A "Christmas in July," complete with sales on a few select front-store items.

Holly handed Rosanna the three white prescription bags. "Did you have any questions today on those medicines?"

"Nee, denki, dear. We've had them all before, as you know."

Holly told Rosanna the total, and the middle-aged woman paid her in cash. At least this customer had returned despite the store having been closed for a few days and being a mess to navigate until the last forty-eight hours.

After saying goodbye to Rosanna, Holly looked up at the Rhythm Clock hanging on the wall. Twenty till seven, almost Greene's closing time. Good. Brandon stood at his station, working on the daily legal paper-work. She still had time to finish inputting the prescriptions that customers would come for tomorrow morning, and then she could go on her Friday night date with Josh.

The door chimed as her customer left. Holly could now see her sister on a ladder leaning across the new front door to drape a garland covered in fake snow over the doorframe. Hopefully Ivy's decorating wouldn't bother any of their Amish customers. Holly had never heard a complaint from them about the decorations. Then again, Greene's had never before decorated for Christmas in July.

Holly still had the same questions she'd had for weeks: What was bothering Ivy, and why wasn't she telling Holly about it? Usually when Ivy decorated or cleaned the pharmacy, she did so with a song on her lips and a wide smile across her face. She seemed so . . . off. And it couldn't be about the car hitting Greene's. During the past several weeks, the Swartzentruber brother had taken over the milking chore that Ivy hated. And as far as Holly knew, Ivy hadn't dated anyone or ended any relationships. So what was the deal? Holly had tried to ask Mamm once, but Mamm had changed the subject in a way that discouraged asking again. So she hadn't. She and Ivy used to talk every Saturday night for hours until they fell asleep. Between work, night school, and time with Josh, Holly and Ivy hadn't spent a Saturday night like that in six months. She'd make sure it happened tomorrow night. Surely her little sister would tell her everything then. *Focus and finish the scripts.* She could think about only one thing at a time, and it was critical that she be accurate when entering prescriptions into the computer. It'd taken her years to get fast and accurate with her typing, but now it came easier than writing with a pen.

The front door chimed again. Holly didn't look up but continued typing the medication's detailed instructions. As her fingers moved swiftly over the keyboard, she checked back and forth between the script and the computer screen to make sure she had it right.

She finally glanced up to see an older Amish man with a long gray beard staring at her. "Good evening." She kept typing. "How can I help you today?"

"I'm Stephan, the bishop for Joshua Smucker's district, Shady Valley Amish."

Oh. She immediately stopped typing — and even breathing. This was *not* what she expected at the end of a long Friday shift.

"H . . . hallo. I'm Holly. Glad to meet you." Was she glad to meet him? It would've been nicer if this meeting had happened in a different setting, like Joshua's farm or at church.

He looked around the pharmacy. "Joshua suggested I stop by and see this pharmacy that an Old Order member is so passionate about working for."

She laughed, hoping she didn't sound too nervous, and held out her hands. "Well, here we are."

Ivy was hanging off a ladder, stringing Christmas lights. *Good grief.* Was it possible he came in the side entrance and hadn't noticed her?

"You like working here?" He sounded confused, but his eyes were focused on the shelves of medicine, not on Ivy.

"Ya. Lyle and Brandon are good pharmacists." She waved at Brandon, who was still at his station and giving her the usual look when he was trying to decide if he should step in with a customer. "We get to help all sorts of people here at Greene's."

"That's good for now, but after you're married, you don't really want this kind of stress on you, ya? Wouldn't you rather leave that to Joshua while you're raising babies?"

His words about her having Josh's babies

made her cheeks warm. "I certainly look forward to having a family with Josh and everything else related to God, marriage, and the Amish community, but I also feel led to help others through medicine."

"Led?"

"My heart longs to continue helping people get well and understand the importance of the medications prescribed to them."

He seemed unsure, but he nodded. "Holly, I admire your bishop, Benuel Detweiler, and respect his decisions regarding your work as an unmarried woman, but I have to say, what I see today gives me pause about your marriage plans."

What? Pinpricks ran hot over her skin, and her head spun. The sound of glass breaking made everyone turn in that direction to see Ivy with a gold-and-silver garland wrapped around her neck. She held up both hands. "It's okay. Remain calm. I dropped a glass ornament. That's all."

Holly's mouth was so dry she could hardly speak. She pressed her hands down the front of her black apron and counted to three. "I'm sorry. Can you tell me what you mean exactly?"

He pointed at Holly's computer. "You're using that thing like an expert. And" — he motioned toward Ivy, shaking his head — "there's another Old Order woman putting *Christmas* decorations in the window in the middle of summer. I was under the impression from Joshua that this store was more in line with our ways. It seems to me like a very worldly place."

It's a modern pharmacy, she wanted to exclaim, but she chose a calm tone and gentle words. "I'm sorry. It does look that way at first, but the decorations are to catch people's attention and alert them that our pharmacy is indeed open and back to business as usual. You may have heard that a car ran into the front of the store three weeks ago."

He nodded.

She tried to swallow but failed. "We use computers in the pharmacy to allow our pharmacists to catch more errors and to easily file our Englisch patients' medications with their insurance companies."

He nodded a few more times. "Holly, I'm glad I came in today. I'll pray for you. God will guide you on what you need to do." With his hands in his pockets, he turned and walked out the store's side entrance.

Holly stared at her computer, not really seeing the words on the screen. *What just happened?* Somehow things were looking even worse for her and Josh. Before they were dating, she'd worried about her bishop's reaction, but Benuel had been gracious. He'd seen the value of what Greene's — and Holly — brought to the Amish districts in the area.

"Something I can help with?" Brandon walked over to Holly's station.

"No, afraid not. That was Josh's bishop. He's not happy with my plan to continue working after Josh and I marry this December."

"But you said that your bishop approves."

"Ya."

"Then I don't understand the problem. You're all Old Order Amish."

She looked up at Brandon. Wearing that clean white coat, he reminded her of a younger Lyle. She and Brandon had been kids when she started working for Lyle and his wife, Beverly. Last year Brandon had achieved his goal of becoming a pharmacist. Could Holly still achieve her goal to become an LPN without having to sacrifice the beautiful life she wanted to build with Josh?

"I know you don't understand." She ran her fingers over the keyboard. "Unfortunately, my bishop has to stay out of the way of Josh's bishop, giving room for the man to come to his own conclusions — whatever that final decision is."

In the front of the store, Ivy climbed down from her ladder and then closed it. "Holly, I'm all done, so I'm going to head out. See you at home later."

"Sure. Thanks, Ivy." It was past closing time now.

As Ivy opened the door to leave, Julie and Josh walked in. His face lit up when he saw Holly, and her heart raced. If only they could go back to their normal, planned date instead of talking about this. She corrected her attitude. This was life, and she couldn't avoid telling him what his bishop had said. Would Stephan change his mind?

Holly opened the gate that separated the prescription-filling area from the over-the-counter store. She went through the gate and walked across the shop to the front door.

"Hi. So someone came by today . . ."

"Ya, Bishop Stephan. I saw him as he was walking down the sidewalk, and he stopped to talk to me."

Holly stepped between Josh and Julie and then locked Greene's front door. The only silver lining to the car accident was that the antique lock had been replaced with one that was easy to bolt.

"Bishop problems?" Julie gave Holly a side hug.

"Probably nothing unexpected, right?" Josh hugged Holly's other side.

Holly took a centering breath. They could get through this. She had Josh, good friends like Jules, Brandon, and Lyle, and a supportive family and bishop. She squeezed both of their shoulders, and then they released the hugs.

Holly noticed a few over-the-counter medicines that were askew and bent down to fix them. "We're having some issues with the Amish rules regarding me continuing to work after marriage, but that's how family works. We have to balance expectations from our order with our own dreams. These things often have to be navigated and negotiated." Well, they were navigated and negotiated for men. She knew of no married women who'd been allowed to bend the rules when it came to work.

She stood and saw Brandon locking the gate to the prescription filling area and arming the alarm. He crossed the store and gave Julie a kiss on the forehead. Holly smiled. Brandon and Julie were taking things slowly, but the two of them made a cute couple and were great partners in health care.

"We good to go on closing?"

"Yep, all set. Jules and I are going to the diner. You and Josh want to come along?"

Holly met Josh's eyes, and he gave a little nod. "Ya, we can start with that. Josh and I were going to get some food and take a walk."

They all stepped outside, and Holly re-locked the door. The sun was low enough that the worst of the heat had broken for the day. A lovely evening for a walk. "I guess I haven't shared a lot of the issues we're dealing with regarding my working after marriage, not even with Mamm and Ivy."

Julie adjusted the strap on her bag as they started walking toward the diner. "If it would help, Holly, once you're living on the farm with Josh, I can pick you up on my way to the clinic and take you home. Then you won't have to hire a driver after you move. It's less than ten minutes from my house, and my little car gets excellent gas mileage."

"Thank you. That's very kind. It'd certainly save us a lot of money and hassle. But the real issue is our order typically doesn't approve of a married woman having a career outside the home. My bishop has been unusually understanding."

Josh took her hand and squeezed it. "And mine holds firm to the traditional values."

Brandon scratched his head. "Holly's family has a farm with plenty of room. Couldn't you move in with her once married?"

"Josh can't leave his farm or parents. His Mamm has diabetes, which she's still adjusting to, and he and his Daed run their free-range egg business. There's a reason you've never heard of a farmer living twenty miles away from his farm. He has to be there, just like you can't go to the hardware store down the street and fill prescriptions for people. He has to keep the flock safe from predators like foxes and safe from sudden storms rolling in, and —"

"Got it. But couldn't you" — Brandon looked upward as he paused — "rent a house just over the district line from where his farm is and move the chickens?"

Holly shook her head. Maybe working as a pharmacist all day, solving medication and insurance issues, had put Brandon in a fixing mood, but there wasn't an obvious solution to this problem. "Josh's family has had a chicken farm on that land for generations. Egg-laying houses are expensive to build, and should his family leave everything they've already built to start fresh because *one bishop* disagrees with me working? No."

They arrived at the door to the diner, and Brandon held it open. "That one bishop is sure being a thorn in your side."

It was a seat-yourself place that they'd been to multiple times over the past few months. The familiar aromas of toasted bread, bacon, and coffee hit her nose as she entered the restaurant. Still holding Josh's hand, Holly crossed the black-and-white-checkered tile floor. She released his hand as she and Josh slid onto the bench of their usual booth.

Holly adjusted her apron. "Josh's bishop isn't being a pain on purpose. He was polite and pleasant. It's his job as bishop to make sure everyone holds on to the Old Ways. If they don't, in a generation those ways will be gone, and we'll fade into the rest of society."

Julie and Brandon sat down on the bench across the table.

"Makes sense." Julie tapped her fingertips on the table. "From what I've seen, the Amish believe that family and community should reflect God's ways, and a wife taking care of just the children and the home is the easiest way to make that work."

Josh folded his hands on the table. "Women are the backbone of our society in many ways. They sacrifice a lot of themselves, especially after marriage."

Holly smiled at him. He was such a good

man. She loved him more than she could say. "There's no easy solution to this, but I'd like to pray about it. Would you two mind joining us?"

Brandon and Julie clasped their hands together on the table. "We'd be honored."

Everyone bowed heads.

Holly closed her eyes. Would the bishop's heart soften concerning a woman working outside the home?

If Josh's bishop didn't change his opinion, how would she possibly choose between giving up her dream of bringing health care to her Old Order community, after all she'd gone through to get to this point, and marrying the perfect man for her, the one she longed to spend her life with and build a family with?

God, I can't see the right path to take, but I know You can.

ELEVEN

The July night air was thick with humidity as Arlan descended the carriage house steps. The sounds of summertime filled the air: cicadas, tree frogs, crickets, and an incessant mockingbird. But Arlan was used to the season's hot weather and the critters' chorus drifting through the open windows. No, the bugs, birds, and frogs weren't what had kept him awake in the middle of the night.

He walked to the closest barbed-wire fence and peered into the pasture. All the clutter in his mind moved to a single conversation he'd had with Betty eighteen hours ago. She'd asked him to stay on until mid-December, saying she needed his help for two reasons: to free up her time so she could focus on preparing for Holly's wedding and to get the homestead ready to host hundreds of guests for the daylong event in December.

He'd taken that opportunity to do as Ivy

had asked and talk to Betty about the workload of increasing the herd. She'd nodded and thanked him, but he wasn't at all sure she took any of it to heart. She'd offered him thirty percent of the milking profits if he continued doing repairs and other chores throughout each day as he'd been doing.

And he'd accepted. *Why?* Why was he still here? It'd been almost four weeks since the wreck, and he didn't know if Magda would be ready to go home even by mid-December, but leaving by then was his goal because now he'd given his word he'd stay. Had the money lured him? Or the freedom this place afforded Magda and him? Or the fact that a widow's firstborn was marrying and she needed his help?

How would he explain to his parents that he'd stayed here until mid-December? The Old Order had a lot going for them, which totally messed with his mind. They weren't as skilled at obeying God as the Swartzentrubers, but they worked hard, dressed modestly, and, despite all he'd been taught, he'd seen no sign of them drinking or partying.

Thoughts of his parents were like heavy weights inside his head. It seemed they weren't as godly as he'd believed all these years. Even so, he still wanted to return home with Magda as soon as possible, repent before the church, and move to New York.

His stomach rumbled. *Confusion must stir the appetite the same as working hard.* Betty had made a cake, and he'd had a small slice after dinner. He'd wanted a second piece, but Ivy had been there, so he'd left as quickly as he could. She was opinionated, and since his goal was to be a good guest and keep his thoughts to himself, it seemed wise to avoid her. He walked toward the house. It was pitch black, and she had to be asleep by now.

Betty never locked the doors, so he eased into the kitchen and with the moonlight could see well enough to cut a piece of cake and put it on a plate. He got a fork and dug into the sugary delight. Betty was quite the cook.

Just then a piercing scream came from upstairs. Was that Magda? Arlan bounded up the steps. Another yell filled the air, longer and louder, and then glass broke.

Ivy was hurrying down the hallway with a lantern. "What's going on?"

"Don't you move!" Magda yelled.

Arlan rushed into her room, followed closely by Ivy. The light from Ivy's lantern cast odd shadows, but he saw Magda standing on the bed, clutching a baseball bat. A wide-eyed man was standing beside the bed with his hands up. A shattered drinking glass was on the floor behind him. Had his sister thrown it at the man and hit the wall instead?

"Red?" Ivy moved in closer.

"Ya," the man murmured. "I was planning to surprise everyone." He shook his raised hands. "Surprise," he said softly. He was wise not to do anything that would upset Magda any further.

"Magda," Arlan chided, "what are you doing wielding a bat?"

"Ya," Ivy said. "You should be more like your brother." She moved in closer. "He brought cake."

Arlan looked down. Sure enough, he was still carrying the plate with cake on it. How had it not fallen off?

Still clenching the bat, Magda moved closer to Red. "I woke to find him trying to get in my bed!"

Red kept his hands in the air. "My bed actually."

Magda lunged toward him a bit. Was she in shock or something?

Red raised his hands higher. "Fine. It's yours." He shrugged. "But can I just mention that for more than a month I've been looking forward to and dreaming about sleeping in my — *your* — lumpy old bed?"

Ivy moved between Magda and Red, and she hugged her brother. "Welcome home."

"Ya. I feel welcomed too."

"And you should." Ivy gestured toward the plate in Arlan's hand. "We have cake." Ivy then climbed on the bed with Magda. Ivy also stood on the mattress, and she looked her in the eyes, and whispered to her while stroking her hair.

Ten or fifteen seconds passed before Magda broke eye contact with Ivy, looked at Red, and visibly relaxed. Maybe Magda was on high alert because she feared that her parents or other Swartzentrubers might show up to drag her back home.

Ivy eased the bat from her. "Magda, this is my brother, Ezra. He's named after our Daed, but we call him Red because of his ginger hair and also because he was born around Christmas, like Holly and me. He's been living in Rocks Mill, which is a few hours from here, for the past year. He's hardly had time to visit due to work."

Magda drew a breath. "He's your brother?"

"Ya. And this is his bed." Ivy grinned. "It's fine. You're fine." Ivy waved the bat toward

Red. "If you'd told someone you were coming, this wouldn't have happened."

Red peered behind Arlan, and when Arlan glanced in that same direction, he saw Betty and Holly in the doorway.

Red lowered his hands slowly. "It never dawned on me that it was better not to surprise my family. That they could've given my room to a complete stranger."

Ivy got off the bed and helped Magda get down. "Magda isn't a stranger. I've introduced the two of you, and her brother, Arlan, brought you cake."

Arlan looked down at the cake. This was embarrassing. But where was Red's indignation for being greeted with madness in his own home? And his Mamm's and sisters' anger, for that matter. It was the middle of the night. Chaos was happening. Shards of glass were in the far corner, and they were making wisecracks. Not one person had been scolded for the incident, and no one had quoted a scripture. Arlan couldn't think of a thou-shalt-not Bible verse that was pertinent, but he bet his Daed could've rattled off three or four.

"Red." Mamm elongated his name. "Hi, sweetie." She came into the room and gave him a big hug before releasing him. "Just so you know" — she patted his chest — "this

147

is Magda's room now. So get out."

Red laughed. "Denki, Mamm. Good to see you too."

Betty chuckled. "I'll get you a blanket and pillow for the couch."

"Hey." Holly embraced him. "I'm so glad to see you." She backed up. "But why are you here?"

Red made a face. "Things didn't go as I'd planned."

"You and Emily?" Holly asked.

Red sighed. "Ya. Can I have cake now?"

Betty cinched the belt on her housecoat. "If you've been dreaming of being in your own bed, it sounds like you've known for a while you needed to come home."

He nodded.

"Are you home for good?" Ivy set the baseball bat on the bed.

"I don't intend to live with my mother indefinitely, but, ya, I'm here for a while. Is that a problem?"

"Not for me." Ivy didn't smile, but she looked very pleased, probably because this meant that even after Arlan left, she wouldn't have to start milking cows again.

Mamm tugged on Red's collar. "With Holly's wedding taking place here in December, I've asked Arlan to help get the farm ready."

"We're expecting nearly three hundred guests to feed, all of Josh's big family," Holly said. "So it'd give us more wedding money to work with if you two mowed the hayfields and stored the hay yourselves. Then there would be no need to hire outside help."

"Ya." Red looked at Arlan. "We can do that, right?"

Arlan nodded. "With the two of us, we could take off ten years of aging on this farm pretty quickly."

"Deal." Red held out his hand, and Arlan shook it. "Besides," Red said, "I need the distraction of hard work." He put an arm around his Mamm's shoulders. "Looking back — and I've done a lot of that the last several weeks — I realized I shouldn't have left you and the girls so quickly or stayed gone so long. I'm sorry."

Betty put her arm around his waist. "You believed Emily was the one. You have nothing to apologize for. Kumm." Betty motioned. "Let's not stand in Magda's room and talk. Let's go to the kitchen."

"Sounds good." Red pointed at Arlan's plate with its slice of cake. "We've got milk to go with that. You and your sister are welcome to join us in continuing this family nonsense downstairs. Guaranteed to be a mixture of fish tales, overt honesty, and a good helping of idle chitchat."

"Denki." Arlan had never seen a man stay so calm and be so upfront about what was going on in his life and do all of it with a bit of humor. Who was this guy?

Holly put a housecoat around Magda's shoulders. "Kumm. Some milk and cake will do you good."

Magda glanced at Arlan and left the room with Holly. Betty and Red filed out also.

Ivy stopped beside Arlan. "You dashed up the steps to save your sister with cake in hand. You think Mamm's cake could be used as a weapon if it came to it?"

"Nee. I'm a pacifist." His face felt hot with embarrassment. "My plan was to coax the intruder into eating cake and then hope he choked on it."

Her grin was his reward for coming up with something to add to the silliness of the last few minutes.

"I have to say, your plan sounds more passive-aggressive than pacifist-like — here's a delicious piece of cake. I hope you choke on it." She laughed. "That aside, I'm going to do you a favor and not tell Mamm you think her cake could choke someone."

She took the plate from him and looked longingly at the cake, apparently still being lighthearted.

"Next time there's a skirmish in the house, bring cake *and* milk. What were you thinking?"

"Clearly I wasn't. I apologize."

Obviously Red's family was thrilled he was home. When Arlan returned home, he would get the opposite response — for months, maybe a year.

"About time you apologized." Ivy's eyes met his, and she smiled. "Right?"

"Maybe." He shrugged.

She left the room with his cake. "You coming?"

He lagged behind. When Ivy got to the bottom of the steps, she hurried into the kitchen, and the volume in the house rose. He sat on the steps, watching and listening to the oddity of this family. They talked openly about personal things. In his few minutes of sitting on the steps, he learned more about the thoughts and feelings of this small family than he'd learned in a year of sharing meals with his own family. It dawned on him why he enjoyed writing letters even when he didn't send them. It was his way of airing all he felt, of sharing all that was never shared at any other time.

Red spoke softly for a moment, and Ivy grabbed his hand, lowered her head, and prayed aloud.

Was he still in a Plain home? Or even on planet Earth, for that matter?

He had no doubt that the Zooks had to face sharp differences of opinion and weather hard times too, but he couldn't see them hiding in corners, plotting hypocrisies beyond everyone's back.

He'd never seen anything like this, and his sister seemed mesmerized too. Despite how interesting the interactions were, they also flew in the face of all he'd been taught.

Maybe he should put his foot down and insist that he and Magda leave. But he'd given his word that he would stay to help, and he wanted some time around this Red person. Red was in his home interacting with the women while being open and vulnerable.

Wasn't this how families were meant to be with each other?

For years his gut had said that men weren't supposed to shove all emotion out of sight, come up with a plan, and demand everyone fall in line behind them.

Is this what the Word meant by "abundant life"? To experience the fullness of the heart, mind, and emotions? To give room to all of it in one's own self and in others without trying to suppress or control it?

A desire to write overtook Arlan. He

couldn't talk about this, not like the Zooks were doing, but he could write about it until he felt clearheaded and calmer.

What was happening in this room is what he wanted — to embrace life with honesty and vulnerability.

TWELVE

Ivy poured steaming, fragrant coffee into ceramic mugs that were sitting on a serving tray. Mamm's fresh-out-of-the-oven sourdough coffee cake smelled even better. Bishop Benuel and his wife, Cheryl, were at the old but sturdy wooden table, along with her Mamm, Holly, Red, Arlan, and Magda. Their conversation was lively with laughter interspersed.

Magda stood and joined Ivy at the kitchen counter. "No coffee for me, denki, Ivy. What can I help with?"

Ivy looked across the spacious kitchen. "You could cut the coffee cake, put it on the little plates, and pass it out. The plates are sitting next to the dessert."

"Sure." Magda removed a knife and serving spatula from their drawers. She was so sweet and such a hard worker. It seemed unfair that she and Arlan had needed to run from their own family.

Ivy picked up the tray of coffees, walked to the large table, and started passing them out. The usual nice cross breeze from the open windows was refreshing, and the overcast sky helped the kitchen and dining room to be not so hot, even in late July. Her great-grandfather must've known how to position the house and windows when he built the place so many years ago.

Cheryl patted Holly's hand. "How are things progressing with Joshua's instruction and plans for your upcoming wedding?"

Every person had to go through instruction to join the faith and marry. Most were like Joshua and waited until the summer before they married, but Holly had gone through hers years ago.

Holly fiddled with the cloth napkin in front of her. "Well, he's still going through instruction, but . . ."

Ivy placed a mug of coffee in front of her sister. She and Holly had talked about this for hours two weeks ago, just like their Saturday nights of old. When Holly asked Ivy if something was bothering her of late, it'd been all Ivy could do to hold her tongue. She wanted to tell her sister everything, but Holly had enough on her.

Benuel sipped his black coffee. "You

sound as if you're concerned about something."

Holly sighed. "Bishop Stephan has a great heart, according to all I've heard about him, but he's very old-fashioned. Josh and I are going about our days as if we're going to have our wedding this December, but right now the bishop hasn't decided if we can marry. You can probably guess why not. He doesn't want to even discuss our wedding plans until October."

Their bishop nodded. "I know your career path isn't conventional, but I've seen the benefits of it throughout your years of working for Lyle. I know Stephan well. He's a fair-minded person. I'd suggest having a meal, and let's all gather and talk about it. Maybe Stephan and I can have a conversation before the meal and that'll help soften his heart. Still, the fact that he's allowing Joshua to continue instruction speaks of good will."

"Denki." Holly seemed to be speaking both to Benuel and to Magda, who'd just placed a piece of coffee cake in front of her, the bishop, and his wife. "I hope so."

Ivy placed mugs in front of her brother and Arlan and then put the last mug at the empty spot where she'd sit in a moment.

Benuel scooped up a corner of his coffee

cake with his fork. "I remember when you went through instruction at seventeen, Holly. Was that really eight years ago?"

Holly had joined the faith at a young age to show their bishop that her heart was all in even though she desired to get her GED and her licensed practical nurse degree. It'd taken time for Benuel to come around and see the benefits of an Amish woman working in a pharmacy and getting enough education that she could legally give advice and discuss medication with their people.

Mamm stirred some sugar into her coffee. "Ya, eight years. And it's been almost eleven since my Ezra died, if you can believe it." Mamm looked directly at Ivy, and their eyes met. Her Mamm didn't need to speak the question aloud. *Are you really going to leave?*

Ivy had been only fifteen when she watched Holly join the church. Holly was so committed to bringing medicine to the area's Amish communities that she was willing to submit to the full rules of the Ordnung while still a teen.

Benuel turned to Red. "I'm sorry Cheryl and I haven't had a chance to drop by sooner. We're glad to have you back home, Red."

Red stretched his arms back and laced his fingers together behind his head. "It feels good to be home. Did Mamm tell you we're going to build up the dairy herd again?"

Ugh. This again. Ivy stabbed her coffee cake a little too hard, making the fork clink loudly against the plate.

If the bishop noticed, he didn't show it. "She mentioned you and Arlan have a plan."

Red clapped Arlan on the shoulder. "I've known this man for only two weeks, but I can tell you he has the right skills when it comes to cows and dairy farming. Our own little herd is noticeably making more milk, and he's been on the farm only for . . . How long again?"

Arlan's eyes moved to Ivy's and lingered for a moment before he returned his attention to the bishop. "Almost six weeks." He knew how she felt about adding more cows. Why was he doing this?

"Right." Red used his fork to pick up the remaining crumbs of his cake. "And since he's staying until December, think of all the progress we can make. We're getting some cows to replace the ones we gave up, supposedly on loan, after Daed died, and we also intend to acquire some less-than-ideal cows for cheap that Arlan can get into good milking shape."

Would they have *more* cows than they'd had before Daed died? No, no, no, this was *not* the plan! Red wasn't staying, not forever. What if he went back to Rocks Mill and married Emily after all? Or found a new girl in another district or state? And Arlan, sure as the sun, wasn't staying. What would Ivy do when they left Mamm with an even bigger herd of cows to deal with?

She couldn't listen to this conversation and continue to hold her tongue, and with the bishop around it wasn't the time for her to speak up. It seemed clear that Mamm hadn't told Benuel anything about Ivy's plans to leave, which made things easier on Ivy. She stood and started gathering the plates and mugs of those who had finished their snack.

Arlan stood too. "Let me help you with the dishes."

Magda stood. "It's my place, not —"

Arlan barely lifted his hand in a "stay there" motion to his sister. "You've hardly touched your cake. You eat. I've got this, Magda."

Ivy wished they'd both remain at the table and let her fume in peace. "No, I'm fine. You don't have to."

"I insist. Just because I grew up without running water in the sink, it doesn't mean I don't know how to wash some plates and cups." He gathered a few of the dishes that were near him.

The bishop and his wife chuckled, and Red went back to giving more details about the cows.

Ivy walked into the kitchen with her hands full of dishes and plunked them on the counter next to the large double sink.

Arlan came up behind her. "You're mad. Why?" His voice was low enough that no one in the dining room could hear him, especially with a separate conversation going on.

"We've already had this conversation."

"But Red's home now. That changes everything."

Ivy plugged the left side of the sink with the stopper and twisted the hot water knob hard to begin to fill it. "Red is no more staying permanently than you are."

"No, he said —"

"He's grieving over his breakup. Whatever he says his plans are during this time doesn't count for a hill of beans." She squirted a generous amount of liquid soap into the water. "I can't . . . *I won't* dedicate my entire life to milking cows. Or spend months helping Mamm get them all back to wherever you're going to get them from. I have plans . . ." She trailed off. Should she bother sharing with someone who couldn't understand?

He placed the plates he was carrying in the soapy water. "What are your plans, Ivy? It's clear they don't involve farming."

"Nee, they don't." She picked up a sponge from the dish drainer. "I . . . I've started a party-planning business with my Englisch friend Tegan."

He looked at the sink and then the dirty dishes beside it, seeming unsure where to start on the task. "Is she the one I've seen pick you up and drop you off several times since I've been here?"

Ivy moved the faucet to fill the other side of the sink with clean water for rinsing the dishes. "Ya. I'm planning to move into an apartment with her. It's the only way I can do all I need to do to grow the party-planning business." She plunged her hands into the soapy water, washed a plate, and then slid it into the rinse water. "There are clean dish towels in the drawer directly under the drying rack. I'll wash. You dry and stack them on the counter."

He nodded and removed a worn towel from the drawer. He was standing an awkward distance from the sink as if he didn't want to be too close to her.

She stretched her arm and passed him the now-clean plate. "You're not surprised that

I want to plan parties for the Englisch?"

He dried the dish and placed it on the counter. "No, you were plenty clear about your dislike of the Old Ways the first morning I was here." He didn't sound disappointed or judgmental.

She looked out the open window above the sink. The sky had darkened, and it smelled as if it was about to rain.

She passed him another clean plate. "I suppose if I told you my thoughts, it's not like you could think worse of me." And why did that bother her?

He kept up with her pace, and the stack of dishes grew. "I don't think bad of you, Ivy. You're kind and hardworking. I just disagree with you about most things, it seems. But I wouldn't take it personal if I were you, because of late I seem to disagree with myself about most things."

Her eyes met his, and his held a spark for life she hadn't noticed before. She shuddered. "Conflicting thoughts and emotions — ugh."

He grinned. "Ya." He pointed at her. "That's the feeling, isn't it?"

She chuckled and nodded. "But everyone will disagree with me once they know my plan. Still, that doesn't make me wrong any more than your people disagreeing with your actions makes you wrong."

"Maybe so." He barely shrugged one shoulder.

"Maybe?"

"Kumm on, Ivy. We can't compare my leaving home with Magda — who was very sick — to your longing to plan parties."

The desire to kick him out of the kitchen grew, and her face flushed hot. Did he have to be so calm and . . . and . . . *right*? She washed the remaining plates in quick succession and passed each toward him, not looking at his face as he took the dishes from her. There were only eight people eating coffee cake. Why were there many more plates than that to wash and lots of flatware?

He stacked each plate with a gentle clink. "That aside, and regarding the cows, you might not think much of it, but this farm could have real value. Your brother and I like the idea of being able to make money while we're here. And if your Mamm wanted to sell the farm one day, with our planned updates it might be more appealing to a buyer, especially to a hobby farmer who doesn't intend for the farm to be the main source of income. At the least it couldn't hurt for everything to be in good running order. Maybe the Troyers of Troyer Yogurt and Cheese would be interested in this

163

place, or maybe another young man would be interested in living above the carriage house and working here with your Mamm if everything was in good shape to begin with."

"You've really thought this through, haven't you?"

"I have, and I'm pretty sure your Mamm shouldn't have to sell her home in order to let you follow your dreams."

Was she pushing her Mamm to do something Mamm didn't want to do? All this time Ivy had believed that the dairy farm was a burden Mamm couldn't enjoy but was holding on to because of a weird sense of love and duty to Daed. Had her own selfishness caused her to ignore what Mamm really wanted?

"I'll be here with your family for a while. It's five months until December, when Magda's baby will be born. I don't know Red's long-term plans, but he's not leaving anytime soon either. Let us work on the herd. I won't leave you with a mess. I'm committed to stay and get the new herd and the old farm running smoothly. I'm not going to leave until you have hired help to replace me, I promise."

She stopped washing a coffee mug and studied him. Maybe she was too close to the situation and too busy trying to get Mamm situated so she could break free. Still, the situation with the cows had a good chance of landing in Ivy's lap when all things were done. "Fair enough. But you're still imposing a future on a home that you're only visiting." She rinsed the mug and passed it his way.

He dried it and set it next to the plates. "Maybe I'm not seeing everything right, but are you sure you are? I can't believe you're willing to leave all this to plan parties. Aren't you allowed enough freedom without needing to leave?"

She should've known it'd come back to this. She took her wet hands out of the sink and dried them on her apron. "Look, you've had four silos full of rules on you your entire life, and now that you're down to two, you think this is freedom."

He turned to look her in the eye. "Everything has rules, Ivy. But can anything else give you what exists right here among your people?"

The simplicity of his words hit with force. He had a way of looking at things that left her speechless. She shrugged, hoping to finish this task in silence. Once done washing the flatware and mugs, Ivy dried her hands on the kitchen towel. "Denki for the help."

"You're welcome." He hung his towel on a peg. "Oh, I need to ask a favor." He reached in his pocket. "Would you put this in the mail for me?" He handed a small white envelope to her. "Your Mamm gave me a stack of paper to write on when I arrived, but I don't have a stamp."

"So this is the girl, right? Lorraine?"

"Ya, that's her."

Ivy waved the letter at him. "Well at least I know you won't always be here, bringing in cows, stirring up trouble, and daily adding more manure to this farm and my life."

He laughed.

She tucked the letter in her dress pocket. Their conversation had confused her. Even when they disagreed, it was nice talking to him, but his points made it even harder to leave her Mamm. At least the letter in her pocket was some assurance that he'd move on. And so would she.

Thirteen

With a wood-splitting maul in hand, Arlan set a small log on the stump, spotted a crack, and aimed for it with the maul. The wood split in two. He tossed the smaller piece on the growing woodpile and split the larger piece again.

The afternoon breeze had plenty of summer heat, but the aroma it carried hinted that fall was coming. Throughout summer he always looked forward to the arrival of September, and today was that day. The heat hadn't relented, but the shadows were growing longer, and it was just a matter of weeks before refreshment arrived. The nights were already cooler.

The letter in his pocket weighed on him, just as it had for a month. He leaned the splitting maul against a log and pulled out the letter. Lorraine's perfect penmanship was easy to read, so the words were clear, but he read it again, hoping to see something he'd missed the first umpteen times. He'd become compulsive about skimming it every hour. Something was off, as if God was trying to tell him something beyond what could be seen on the page.

Dearest Arlan, I'm disappointed in the position you've put me in. I either have to betray you or the church. Please rethink what you're doing. Magda is young and unmarried, and her desires can't dictate your decisions. You need to return to your community and do right by your parents before you ruin us. We've waited so long to be together, and it can happen now. You should be making plans to move here, not hiding your sister. I've told no one where you are, but I'm begging you to rethink this. As it stands, you've made me a part of your lies and deception too.

He stared at the words, searching for answers. Her overreaction was his fault. He should've written a series of letters and eased into the part about Magda being pregnant.

Maybe they could return home now. It was likely their parents were ready to accept Magda's condition without insisting she do things their way. But for reasons Arlan was unsure of, he had no burning desire to try to set things right with his Daed or the bishop.

Magda was thriving here. Arlan needed to write to Lorraine again and this time focus on easing her concerns, but how?

"Hey." Ivy's voice startled him. She had a tray with a sandwich and lemonade.

He closed the letter and put it in his pocket. "Hi."

"Mamm sent me, saying that you didn't come in for lunch and that dinner is simply leftovers and sandwiches."

He was never sure how he felt about Ivy. He liked her outspoken ways and sense of humor, and she was nothing like he imagined someone leaving for the world would be. She seemed respectful of her Mamm, who was kind, lenient, and giving. So why wasn't being here enough for her?

She put the tray on the stump. There was a perfectly good picnic table on the other side of the yard, and he wanted to ask her to sit there with him. But realizing that was what he wanted bothered him, so he turned two logs upright for seats, grabbed the sandwich and lemonade, and sat.

Ivy remained standing. "Do you ever stop moving during the day?"

"Daylight is a gift." He shrugged. "And

our ancestors lived that way."

"They did." Ivy sat on the upturned log. "It's admirable, but for them it was also absolutely necessary. We have a choice."

"Or in your case, the choice has you." Arlan swallowed another bite of the sandwich.

Ivy pinned him with a hard stare. "Um, change of subject." She interlaced her fingers and cupped them over her knees, looking relaxed. "So you said you enjoy reading fiction?"

He chuckled, and it surprised him. Despite her desire to leave the Amish, she was a very diplomatic and interesting woman. "I do, at least I think I do. Your Mamm gave me some books off her shelves, and those haven't been too interesting."

Ivy chuckled. "I guess not. If they came from Mamm's bookshelves, they're classified as women's fiction, meant for women."

"Women's fiction?"

Ivy's eyes danced, but she stopped short of actually laughing. "What *do* you enjoy reading?"

"I only have five books. I dug them out of a garbage bin years ago and kept them hidden in the hayloft." He'd never told anyone about that. "But they're fantastic every single time I read them. *The Count of Monte Cristo, Oliver Twist, Robinson Crusoe,* the

170

Adventures of Huckleberry Finn, and *Johnny Tremain.*"

"Got it. You like adventure, male centric. Probably would prefer historic settings to contemporary. I'll see what I can dig up."

"You might have some here?"

"Definitely. Daed loved to read a good adventure story."

"Really?" Was she teasing him?

She studied him, those blue eyes filled with earnestness. "Didn't any of the men in your district read fiction?"

Arlan shook his head. "Nor the women, although after seeing what women's fiction is all about, I'm not sure I blame them."

Ivy chortled. "They may not be male adventure, but they're good reads, and you know it."

Her laughter was contagious, and he felt humor stir inside him. "I may know it, but you can't make me fess up to it."

"True." She held up her hands in surrender. "Not interested in making you do anything. Some of my fondest childhood memories are of my whole family sitting in the living room every night, reading various books. Even after we could read ourselves, Daed would read aloud to us, and then we'd talk about it. Now those were lively conversations. I haven't read the five you mentioned, or we could tell each other what we think."

"Since I've read them, how about I summarize the stories and *tell* you what to think about each part?"

She laughed again, and he realized how beautiful her laughter was. "What would be the fun or frustration of that?"

"Who needs fun or frustration?" he teased.

" 'A merry heart doeth good like a medicine,' so there's your answer for why to have fun. And in those moments of frustration over someone's opinion, our way of thinking is being challenged and broadened. It's a beautiful thing."

How could someone so balanced in their thinking and emotions want to leave her people? "Hey, Ivy, if frustration over other people's opinions is so beautiful, let me share with you —"

"Nee." She stood. "Let's end this conversation on a good note."

But he was curious why she was so intent on leaving her home. Was he missing something? "Could I ask you a question about your plans to leave?"

She sat. "It's likely to ruin these few moments of good vibes we have going."

"Ya, but I need to know."

"Then ask."

"Your Mamm is kind and lenient. From what I've heard, your bishop is a fair man in every way. Under those circumstances don't you think you're wrong to leave the Amish?"

"I don't. No." She shook her head. "If your life had the kind of freedom you needed, you wouldn't be here. If my life had the kind of freedom I need, I wouldn't have to break with my family to pursue an honorable dream. But I do have to, and it eats at me on the inside." Her voice broke as she knotted her fist and tapped her chest. "I shouldn't have to disappoint or hurt anyone to live in an upstanding Englisch home or room with my Englisch friend or be a party planner for weddings, bachelors, bachelorettes, moms-to-be, and children's birthdays."

"I'm not sure a person needs all those festivities."

"I get that. I'm not always sure the client needs all of that either. Some spend five to six hundred dollars for a child's birthday. But then I remind myself that maybe it's the one thing that child or parent needs to get through the upcoming days."

"They can't *need* it. It's a party, for Pete's sake."

"You realize that's judgmental, right?"

"I'm just saying it how it is."

"No. It's judgmental, and we both know that Jesus tells us not to judge."

"How does one not see a situation for what it is?"

"Judging says, 'Your leaving is wrong! I can give you a long list of why it's wrong, and if you follow through, you'll pay the price for sure!' Assessing says, 'You're leaving, and I'm concerned it may be wrong. Maybe my concerns are just my fears coming out, but I'd like to share my thoughts, and you can decide which is right.'" She shrugged. "See the difference?"

"Okay." This was an interesting conversation. Serious, yet he felt lighthearted, as if they were teasing their way to truth. This was definitely new territory for him. "I assess that party planning may be a colossal waste of money and that it may teach people, especially children, that they are the center of the universe."

"Better. Still leaning toward judgmental but a clear improvement. So think about this." She stretched her legs out and crossed her ankles. "About a month before my Daed died, he took me to an ice cream stand, and he let me choose whatever flavors of ice cream I wanted. He said it was 'I love Ivy day,' and he didn't want me to forget it."

Her eyes filled with tears, and she took a deep breath. "The server put each scoop in a container so big" — she gestured with her hands several inches apart — "that no child needed that much. Not any child. We sat at the picnic table while I ate and talked nonstop in my excitement. Looking back, I realize he didn't care what any onlooker thought of my enormous dish of ice cream. On the days I felt as if I was going to die from the grief of losing him, the memory of that day eased my mind, bringing comfort, and I could breathe again."

"Okay." Arlan's vision blurred with tears. He rubbed his eyes with his palms, unable to believe all he felt. "Parties for everyone. Huge ones." He stretched his arms out. "Whatever the parents want. It's not my place to judge."

Ivy grinned. "Exactly." She raised one hand toward him, but he had no idea why. She grabbed his wrist and slapped his palm against hers. "It's called a high five."

He raised his brows.

"It's a thing, evidently not for Swartzentrubers."

"The Swartzentrubers are right about not doing *that* one thing if nothing else."

Ivy laughed. "High fives? Maybe so. Speaking of parties and events, I'm coordinating a fall festival for the end of October for a preschool, and I'm going to need some muscle."

"Sure. Not a problem." He set his empty glass on the tray. "Denki for the food." He jammed the splitting maul into the log on the stump so no one would trip over it. "Polka Dot has been missing for a few hours. Since it's time for her to drop her calf, I best go look for her." Ivy had been asking him about Polka Dot every day all week long. "Would you like to walk with me?"

She blinked and then smiled. "I'd like that."

When they reached the cattle gate, he opened it and held it for her, but as she entered, he heard the crunching of gravel under tires, probably car tires. "You expecting someone?"

Ivy shook her head. "Let's see who it is. It could take a while to find Polka Dot, and I wouldn't want to make someone wait for us to return."

"I like your logic" — he held the gate as she came back through — "except when you mix in a whole lot of emotions." He fastened the gate tight.

"Me to a T." She chuckled. "You think intelligently until a whole lot of judgment floods in. Try remembering the verse in Galatians that says it is for freedom that Christ has set us free."

Arlan mulled over her words as they strode toward the house. He saw a large van, the kind that carried families of Amish. A moment later he spotted Lorraine next to the vehicle, and her parents were with her.

Even if he did think intelligently, none of it was at work right this moment. His brain seemed frozen.

"Arlan?" Ivy shook his arm.

He realized he'd stopped cold. "It's my girlfriend and her parents."

"Oh." Ivy nudged him forward. "Go," she whispered.

Arlan swallowed hard and hurried toward them. Betty was outside and meeting his parents by the time he walked up. He nodded. "Hallo."

The jangle of Pennsylvania Dutch words coming at him from all three of them at once was overwhelming. But Lorraine had all his attention. They'd not seen each other in two years, and this wasn't the way he'd envisioned their meeting again.

"Die entsetzlich Druwwel Du duscht." She gazed into his eyes, looking earnest.

He hadn't expected her first words to him would be "The awful trouble you do."

"Kumm. Loss uns schwetze."

Lorraine looked at her Daed for approval when Arlan asked her to come with him and talk.

He nodded. "Ya."

Arlan spoke to Lorraine's parents and shook her Daed's hand. Betty invited the parents inside, but they asked to sit at the picnic table, saying it was a beautiful day. The driver sat in the vehicle with the engine running, and her parents weren't going inside, so they didn't intend to stay long.

Just beyond earshot Lorraine stopped walking. "Arlan." She bit her bottom lip and smiled up at him. "I have good news. I talked to my Daed. He's worked out a deal with your bishop and mine. If you and Magda get in the van right now, we can go to your house and ask forgiveness from your parents and church leaders. Then you can ride back with us to the New York community immediately afterward. You can stay with your brother if he's willing, but my older brother has agreed for you to stay with him while you get your feet under you."

That was quite an agreement she'd worked out. How had she managed it? Far more important, why wasn't he even a little excited at the idea of going to New York immediately?

"What kind of trouble will Magda be in?"

"She'll return home, where she belongs. She'll be fine. Of course her life won't be as smooth and easy as yours. Her sin is what caused you to leave with her, and she'll have to answer for that."

"So I get off scot-free. Nee, I'm rewarded for my sin by being allowed to move to New York sooner than before, and Magda will be punished?"

She shooed a fly away from her face. "You have a good heart. It's big and kind, and it's why I've always wanted to marry you, but Magda's sin is hers to bear. It's not yours to carry for her or your duty to run with her so she can avoid the wisdom of your parents."

Were those her words or her parents'?

He picked up several small rocks from the gravel driveway and threw one down the lane. "My actions seem rebellious and foolish. I know they do, but Magda was so sick, and she needed —"

"Okay, but what's done is done. You need to think about what you're doing now."

Lorraine sounded different from the girl he remembered.

"You need to do as your parents and community want before they refuse to let you join the church or move to New York. This nonsense could destroy us. How could you put me in this position?"

He hadn't told her about his parents' plans to take the baby from Magda and raise it as their own. That would mar his parents' reputations, and he wouldn't do that.

"Lorraine, hear me out, please." He told her how sick Magda had been and how unfair his parents were to her when she needed help and how Magda didn't deserve to be punished. "Love forgives, and it keeps no record of wrongs. We should feel compassion for Magda."

"What?" She shook her head. "I feel angry, and you should too. It was wrong, and you let her off 'scot-free,' as you worded it."

"She's not free. She's already paid a stiff price, and she'll continue to pay for years and years. She may never find someone to marry after this, and she's given up what few opportunities would have been available to her in order to keep this baby. Everyone knows her sin. She doesn't need our anger as well."

She scoffed. "She's paying the consequences for coming up pregnant, but that's not the same as being disciplined for her disobedience."

The Lorraine he thought he knew was hidden under a hardness that disappointed him.

He threw another rock as far as he could, releasing some of his pent-up frustrations. "We're not ready to go home. I've made a commitment to this family who has helped us out so much. I need to honor what I said to Betty and stay at least until December."

"That's three months from now! You've disobeyed your family and church, but you intend to keep your word to an outsider? Do I even know you?"

Apparently not, but how could she? He barely knew himself since he'd plowed into the pharmacy. It was as if he'd only begun to read the book describing his childhood and, while reading it, was learning how he'd felt and what he'd thought back when those events unfolded, as well as how he felt about them now. He also believed that writing revealed his inner workings, and it did, but whatever was happening as he continued to stay here was revealing far more.

"Nee, you don't know me, and it's not your fault. We barely knew each other when you moved away."

Their relationship had been mostly stolen glances at each other from across the room. She'd been nineteen when her family moved away and they had promised to marry. He'd thought he was in love with her, but as he stood here today, he knew what he'd been in love with was the hope she represented, the hope of moving away from his parents and into a district that wasn't as strict. He'd always wanted to work a farm, and the whole plan of helping his brother purchase one — although his financial contribution had been small — and moving to a new state had bolstered his hope. Having a girl to marry completed his hope. But now he realized Lorraine had represented hope for his future, and that's what he kept writing to — hope. Not Lorraine. He'd thought he looked forward each day to writing to her, but what he'd really enjoyed was the writing itself. It helped him process his thoughts and emotions. He'd realized this rather vaguely after arriving here when he wrote to her but didn't mail those letters. The joy of writing had been the same.

"Lorraine." He wanted to promise her that he'd return home when his commitment here was done, but the words refused to leave his mouth. "I'm not going home right now. I can't."

"Don't you want to marry me?"

Arlan's heart thudded. "I'm sorry. I really am, but we never should've talked so freely of marrying when we barely knew ourselves, much less each other." He angled his head, trying to catch her eye. "I'm sorry, Lorraine."

She turned away from him and strode back toward her parents. Wasn't that an odd response? Was hardness all she had? Shouldn't there be some emotion and strong words slung at him?

Maybe this was who she was. Exacting. Her way or no way. Or maybe she was no more in love with him than he was with her.

Had they both been in love with the idea of marriage? In love with the dream and hope of marriage? As confusing as his internal life was since he entered his teen years, he'd always wanted three things: to know God, to have a family of his own someday, and to farm. For years he thought the answer to all that was moving to New York and joining the Swartzentruber Amish there.

Hope crumbled, and nothing made sense. Had he deluded himself all this time? His head spun, feeling the earthquake and its aftershocks.

As hard as this moment was, he braced himself for what had to be said to her family. He followed Lorraine to the picnic table, with everyone watching his every move as he approached.

The wind picked up, smelling of rain, and thunder rumbled in the distance. Before too long, hopefully before a thunderstorm moved in, he needed to find Polka Dot and her new calf. But right now he had to focus on talking to Lorraine's parents. If all he knew was his people's teachings of what was right and wrong, he wouldn't have the courage to break his word to Lorraine's family. He would cave under the thoughts of the sinfulness of his actions. But he'd dug those fiction books out of the garbage all those years ago, and despite how blasphemous it felt, he drew courage from the pools of thought he found in those books. In them made-up people expressed honest thoughts because real people who'd experienced life outside of Swartzentruber life had poured out their hearts in the books. He drew strength for this moment even from the overzealous freedom-seeking Ivy. She might be missing the mark by miles, but at least she was willing to stand up for what she wanted.

Arlan stopped near the table, and the Zooks excused themselves and went inside. Movement at a window in the Zook home caught his attention, and he saw Magda peeping out from behind a curtain. She had to be terrified, and he wanted to smile and nod, assuring her it would be all right, but he thought it best not to draw attention to her presence.

"I'm sorry for the emotional turmoil you feel over me being here, but I'm not leaving at this time. In fact, not for months yet. I will return and do whatever it takes to set things right with my family and community, but Lorraine and I have talked, and we're no longer planning to marry."

Her Daed stood, got right in his face. "You're a wolf in sheep's clothing, and I'm glad to know that now!"

Arlan held the man's gaze. "Again, I'm truly sorry for how this feels and the struggle you'll have to accept and forgive me."

A clamor of voices rose. Her Daed didn't back down, saying a lot that Arlan didn't actually hear. But he heard enough. They would notify his parents where Arlan and Magda were before the day was through.

Then they climbed in the van, slammed the doors, and were gone.

Should Arlan and Magda pack up and leave?

FOURTEEN

Thunder rumbled, and rain pitter-pattered against the screen of the open window. Boxes were now everywhere in Ivy's bedroom, and she still hadn't found what she was looking for. She crawled farther back in the closet and pointed the high beam of the flashlight into the recesses. Light from candles and kerosene lanterns was annoyingly insufficient when trying to see in dark spaces.

Finally she spotted a torn, dented box marked "Daed's favorite books." She dragged it out, found a space on her bedroom floor not filled with boxes, and knelt.

The moment she opened the box, her Daed's deep, calm voice filled her mind and heart with lines from a dozen books. She could see his expression change and hear his voice lower to a whisper and then get loud as he read, drawing his family in, making them feel as if they were Brian from

Hatchet or Lucy from *The Chronicles of Narnia* or Travis from *Old Yeller.* How many long winter nights had they spent in the living room in front of a roaring fire, listening to him read? During the other seasons they had raised the windows, and even now she could smell the aromas and see the beauty of spring, summer, and fall outside the window while he read about lives and lands she could only imagine.

Her heart ached for her Daed, and tears filled her eyes. It hit her why she'd boxed up his favorite reads and put them out of sight. Hiding the books hadn't helped at all for several years. Still, she kept them in the dark, hoping it would make a difference. Eventually it did . . . or seemed to. What else had she boxed up and slid into dark corners?

Party planning had a lot of the same elements as her time with her Daed — families gathered in anticipation and making memories that would last a lifetime. A well-planned party was the closest she could come to reconstructing how she felt during some of the best parts of her life.

"Ivy?" Holly called as she tapped on the door.

"Kumm."

Holly entered, and her eyes moved across

the scene of strewed boxes to Ivy, whose unpinned hair had to be a mess after she'd crawled into the closet half a dozen times. Without a word Holly walked over to Ivy and knelt on the floor beside her. She reached into the box and ran her fingertips across the covers. Her sigh was also a faint moan. Grief and beautiful memories lived inside this box.

Ivy pulled out various books, looking for the perfect one to pass to Arlan. She would let him read each one in due time, but he needed a very special one right now. The look on his face an hour ago as the Zooks went inside, leaving him to talk to Lorraine's family, had pricked her heart.

"I'm looking for a perfect book to help Arlan through the next few days."

"Ivy . . ." Holly cleared her throat. "I . . . I know you're planning to leave."

Ivy's breath caught, and she couldn't make herself look at her sister. *Breathe.* She drew a slow breath, fidgeting with the pages of *That Was Then, This Is Now.* It seemed an appropriate book to have in hand at this moment. A tale of two best friends, each one following who he was, and in the end they took very different paths. Unfortunately it didn't end well.

"I'm sorry," Ivy whispered.

"You should be."

Ivy looked at her sister, wanting to argue, but tears were threatening.

"You should be sorry that I had to figure out on my own what's going on with you. Do I even have to say it? I'm your sister! I'm here for you. Do you hear me? We need to talk about your plans. We're certain to argue, but for the record I will not let anything, including religion or your personal view of what's right or wrong, come between us."

"Ya?" Tears fell. Ivy set the books down and wiped her cheeks.

"Ya." Holly grabbed Ivy by the shoulders. "I'm yours. You're mine. We'll learn to navigate everything else. Okay?"

Ivy set the books down and hugged her sister. "Denki." She held her tight. "I wanted to tell you, to talk about it, but you have so much on your plate already. Plus, I didn't want you to get in trouble once the community learned about my plans and that you knew." Ivy realized another part of why she'd kept this to herself. "And if you were going to reject me, I wanted to be gone first."

"Some of that was thoughtful, some not. But if that's how you think, you need to stop thinking."

Ivy laughed and sat back, brushing tears off her face. "I needed to be able to ask *you* if I should tell you, but somehow I couldn't make that work."

"Ya, life's funny that way." Holly brushed some of Ivy's hair behind one ear. "You okay?"

Ivy shrugged. "My decision is right for me, but it's a really hard thing to do to Mamm." Ivy was ready to share every bit of how she felt with someone who would truly understand. Tegan couldn't get it. She tried, but in her world it was expected that when children grew up, they followed their hearts and landed elsewhere. As long as they called, texted, and visited regularly, the parents felt fulfilled and satisfied in having launched their child.

A clap of thunder made Ivy jump to her feet. "Polka Dot!" She grabbed a raincoat out of the closet. "She's been missing most of the day, bound to have given birth." She jammed her arms into the ankle-length coat. "Arlan was going to look for her when Lorraine arrived. I doubt he's thought about that cow since."

Holly stood and grabbed a short, lightweight raincoat from the closet.

Ivy looked out the window, seeing sheets of rain against a gray sky. Metal clanked, and she looked for its source. "Look." Arlan had a halter on Polka Dot, leading her into the barn, her new calf trotting behind. "No cow is better than Polka Dot at hiding and wedging herself in a secure spot when calving. He must be a cow whisperer to have found her and coaxed her home, especially in weather like this."

Holly joined her at the window. "He needs to know something I learned from Julie earlier today — Magda doesn't have to go back, minor or not. When Lorraine and her family arrived here hours ago, Magda panicked. So I called Julie, and she explained some things to me. Bottom line: what Magda's parents did in not allowing her medical care isn't legal. She could've died, so with a little legal pushback against their parents, they won't have to worry about them anymore. My guess is a letter from a lawyer or a call from Julie would cause their Daed to drop the whole matter, especially since she turns eighteen next month."

"Why didn't Julie say this earlier?"

"She was trying not to scare them off. Was either one ready to consider having any Englisch authority, including a private lawyer, confront their Daed?"

"Nee," she whispered, "but I think he's

ready now." Ivy was excited to tell him the news and share a good book. She grabbed *The Lion, the Witch and the Wardrobe* from the box, hoping he wouldn't mind that it was a children's book. There were certain books everyone should read, regardless of how old they were when they learned about the books. "Kumm." Ivy gestured for Holly to follow her. "You can explain the legal stuff."

Holly removed the raincoat. "Nee. I was only willing to get out in this yuck to help you." She looked out the window. "You don't need me for this."

Ivy studied the barn. Arlan was inside it now and had lit the kerosene lantern. She put the book inside her coat. "We'll finish talking later. I need advice on how to make my leaving as easy on Mamm as possible."

Holly nodded. "I understand, although I don't agree with your plan. My room. Ten o'clock. Bring cake."

Ivy's eyes filled with tears again. "Denki." Relief that Holly knew her secret strengthened her. Although she realized heated arguments were ahead, she was certain that love and respect would have the final word between them.

FIFTEEN

Holly carried a piping hot dish of chicken potpie toward the back door. Magda was at the sink, washing dishes, and she'd asked not to join their guests, and Holly had agreed. Today was about Holly and her upcoming wedding. A meal with two bishops, each with power over Joshua's and her future, had her twisted in knots.

Her Mamm was behind her, carrying a pitcher of ice water. The sounds of friendly conversation rode on the air. That was a good sign, right? She rounded the corner of the house, and Josh looked up from his conversation with her bishop, Benuel, and his wife, Cheryl. Josh winked at her. What was he thinking to show such a display of affection in front of the bishop? Josh wanted to be by her side and help get the meal on the picnic table, but she'd told him it would be best if he left "women's work" to the women while his bishop was here. Ivy, with a small stack of green cloth napkins in hand, was talking with Josh's bishop, Stephan, and his wife, Mary, as well as Josh's parents. The scene looked friendly and casual, but today — the upcoming mealtime conversation — could sanction or kill her career.

Holly set the dish on the picnic table. Ivy seemed to have excused herself from her small group and was now giving each place setting a napkin. Holly came behind her, placing flatware on the napkins.

Ivy pointed at Holly's hands. "Breathe, Holly. Take a few slow breaths."

Holly looked down to see her hands were shaking. She closed her fists to stop the trembling and took a deep breath. What Josh's bishop said today meant life and freedom to her — or the lack of it. But her mind was made up. She would follow through with her decision regardless of what was said.

"Ya, you're right." Holly paused and breathed deeply again. Nothing of late seemed to calm her as much as smelling the musty scent of falling leaves and feeling the slight crispness that rode on the autumn breeze. She'd been baking and preparing for this meal all day. It wasn't surprising that the October weather was perfect so they could have this dinner outdoors, but it was a nice blessing.

Mamm put her arm around Holly's shoulders. "You'll do great."

Holly nodded, hoping Mamm was right. She caught Josh's eye and gestured at the table, and he asked everyone to take a seat. When their heads were bowed, Holly found it hard not to follow their usual family mealtime practice of speaking out loud to God about what was on their hearts. The traditional silent prayer before the meal no longer came naturally.

After the silent prayer ended, Bishop Stephan dipped food onto his plate. "This looks delicious." He slid the hot dish to Holly's bishop.

Benuel spooned the potpie onto his plate. "It does."

"Holly's a good cook." Mamm passed Stephan a bowl of salad. "And she's very efficient, making the most of every minute, which leaves her time to get everything done in a day."

Her mother's praise was a thinly veiled effort to say that Holly could do all her duties as an Amish wife and Mamm and hold a job outside the home.

Stephan gave a quick nod and then changed the subject to the weather. He followed that by asking Bishop Benuel various things about his church, the people, and even how well the bench wagon that moved the pews from home to home was holding up.

Josh gently squeezed her hand under the burgundy tablecloth, giving the signal he'd told her he would. A squeeze meant that it would be okay, that Stephan's eyes would open to her heart, and that he would accept her need to keep her role as a pharmacy tech. She didn't want to discourage Josh, but she felt the opposite of Josh's prediction would happen.

Bishop Stephan wasn't going to understand Holly's point of view. But his decision would be based on what he felt was right. Holly closed her eyes, praying once again. Were they going to talk about the wedding soon? The dinner conversation was pleasant enough, but Stephan had to know that she and Josh were anxious to hear what he had to say.

Stephan wiped his mouth and looked from Josh to Holly. "Thank you for this meal, Holly. It's been wonderful to get to know you and your family a little better by being here and seeing you on your farm. I'm sure you're waiting to hear my answer about your engagement. I would love for you to join our Shady Valley community. I really would, but I'm afraid I can't sanction your plan to continue working. I've been praying about this ever since I visited you at work almost three months ago. Unfortunately, I have to make unpopular decisions because I can't compromise what I know to be the right way of living. You'll need to quit your job at the Englisch pharmacy if you intend to join my district and live there once married."

There it was. Holly's stomach dropped. But she'd known this was coming.

Bishop Benuel looked disappointed, but he smiled and nodded. "I know this has been a tough decision for you, Stephan, and we appreciate your many prayers that have brought you to this decision."

Josh looked from his bishop to Holly. His handsome brow furrowed, as it always did when he was upset.

Holly fought for composure, trying to keep the tears at bay. Her chin quivered, but she managed a smile. "I understand. Denki for your open heart to our request."

Her eyes met Josh's, and she mouthed, *It's okay.* She held her chin up and looked at her bishop. She'd shared a lifetime of meals with him and his wife on this farm after her Daed died. He and Cheryl had helped the Zook family find a semblance of normalcy again. When Holly came to him to ask about getting her GED, she'd been so nervous she could hardly stay on her feet. He'd been reluctant for a while, and he'd prayed about it for a long time, but he returned to her with a yes. Later she realized she needed an associate's degree in nursing in order to legally share information about medicine. Driving a rig to people's homes to deliver their medicine wasn't enough. She needed to be able to talk to them about the medication. Her bishop spent a long time praying about that too, but again his answer was yes. After that he'd been fully supportive, because he understood why she wanted this so badly. She wanted to prevent any other Amish girl or boy from losing a loved one to something that was preventable with the right information and medicine.

She met her future bishop's eyes. "I've been praying about it too, Stephan." She drew a deep breath, trying to force the words out of her mouth. "I'll put in my resignation at Greene's, effective before the wedding in mid-December."

Ivy choked and pulled the napkin to her mouth, coughing. "What?"

Holly didn't respond to her.

Stephan smiled, as if pleased with one of his children. His shoulders seemed to relax. "Gut. Denki, Holly. We welcome you to our community." His words were warm and filled with relief.

The hardest part was over, but Holly's face was hot, and if she stayed at this table, she'd burst into tears in front of everyone. All those years of hard work, studying, praying, traveling from home to home in a horse and buggy. She was giving it all up. She'd never recover from this decision.

Mamm stood. "How about some apple crisp? The apples are from my cousin's orchard." She passed the potpie dish to Holly, giving her a reason to leave the table quickly.

That was all the opportunity Holly needed. She clutched the dish and walked away from the table as fast as she could without running. She kept walking until she reached the other side of the house and was on the front porch, out of sight of everyone. She sank into the wooden rocking chair. A few tears fell into the almost-empty potpie dish. She'd known for weeks that this moment would come, and yet somehow she couldn't gain control over her raging emotions.

Josh came around the side of the house, walking normally until he, too, was out of sight of the others. He ran up the porch steps and knelt in front of her. "Holly." His brown eyes held determination. "No, no, no, no. We can't agree to this. I told you before we even started dating that I don't want to change you, and health care is such a big part of who you are. You can't quit."

"I can. It's my decision."

"I can't be the reason you have regrets for the rest of your life."

She cupped his face with a hand. "I will never, ever regret choosing a life with you, no matter what I have to give up. If the bishop were demanding this of you, wouldn't you give up your chicken farm?"

"Well, ya, but —"

She put a thumb over his mouth. "What we have is bigger than me being a pharmacy tech and an LPN or you raising chickens. Our love is stronger, and the family we're going to build is worth more than anything else."

Josh stood. "But you're part of the Greene's Pharmacy family too. And your dreams matter just as much as mine. No one is asking me to give up my chicken farm."

Ivy hurried up the porch steps, staring at Holly.

Holly wiped away any remaining tears with the back of her hand. "I'm fine."

"I'm not." Ivy gestured, palms up. "You're

giving up your dreams and the very thing you felt God wanted you to do so they will approve your marriage?" She turned to Josh. "You'd *let* her give this up?"

"Ivy." Holly stood, feeling a bit stronger already. "It's my decision to make. I'm not giving up what God has asked me to do, but I'll do it by being a volunteer. The bishop will have no issue with me visiting our sick people to make sure they're taking their medicines. I will continue to encourage them to visit Greene's and go see Jules at the clinic. But unlike working at the pharmacy, I'll be able to take our babies with me, and that will be just fine with the church."

Ivy clamped her hands on her head. "I can't believe this."

Holly put a hand on her sister's shoulder. "A year ago I would've said the same thing. But if I'm serious about trusting God with my life — and I am — then I have to be willing to follow the Old Ways even when I don't agree with them. Our way isn't easy, but I believe in it."

It wasn't the end of her life or even of her involvement in health care for the Amish. She just had to keep the faith, let go of her disappointment, and create a new dream concerning her work with Greene's.

SIXTEEN

The late-October afternoon breeze rustled Ivy's dress, and she smelled the salty-sweet scent of kettle corn wafting from the fall festival snack tent. Her stomach growled. But there was no time for her or Tegan to grab anything to eat right now.

Raysburg Field was buzzing with adults and children. This spot near Greene's Pharmacy was perfect for a lot of outdoor functions, especially one like today's, with a few event tents set up, a bouncy house, and a petting zoo. People seemed to be really enjoying today.

Ivy focused on the small group in front of her welcoming station. She plucked a yellow balloon from the bunch on the check-in table and handed it to a little boy who looked to be about four. "Here you go. Enjoy!" She nodded at the adults standing behind him, assuming they were his parents. "Welcome to the Primrose Primary School

Fall Festival. The snack tent is over to the left, and it's all free. There's a bouncy house in the middle, and be sure to visit the petting zoo located on the right side of the field. We brought my favorite cow, Polka Dot, and her new baby, Bubbles." She slid a clipboard toward the adults. "If you would please sign in, that'll help us know which families participated today. I'm Ivy. If you need anything, just come find me or my friend Tegan." She motioned to Tegan, who was edging the helium tank closer to the table, probably to be sure no one tripped over it.

"Thanks." The man filled in his name and the number of people in his group. The little boy had bounced up and down when Ivy mentioned the petting zoo.

This preschool was an awesome client for her and Tegan's business because they held at least three big parties every year, starting with the fall festival. Ivy did a quick count of the balloons left in the bunch. Only six remaining balloons. She and Tegan had thought ahead and tied each of them to a small bag of animal crackers so they wouldn't float away. She looked down and skimmed the number of people who'd signed in compared to how many families were part of Primrose Primary School. At least fifteen more students could arrive.

"Hey, Tegan, do you think you could fill seven more balloons for me? I'm going to check on the petting zoo."

"Sure thing." Tegan gave Ivy a small salute with her index finger.

Ivy walked across the grassy field. Holly and Mamm had offered to help her work the snack tent, and they were currently passing out bags of freshly popped kettle corn. But Ivy kept walking because the petting zoo was calling her name.

Her thoughts reeled back to this field last October. Holly had planned a health fair, and a mix-up caused a low turnout. Later Holly, Mamm, and Ivy, with the support of the Amish community, had worked hard to save enough money for Greene's to host another health fair this coming spring. By then Holly's wedding would be behind her, and the weather would be warmer. But Ivy supposed that wasn't going to happen now. How had Holly agreed to give up her pharmacy job after working there for more than a decade? She'd earned her GED, passed the tests to get into nursing school, and begun the process of getting her LPN degree. She was giving up all that? Ivy couldn't fathom it.

She also couldn't imagine being in Arlan's

shoes. Eight weeks ago he had written to his Daed, explaining Magda's legal rights and telling him that they weren't coming home yet. He hadn't heard a word from his Daed since. Magda had turned eighteen last week and now had the legal right to live wherever she chose.

Life seemed to be a series of hard decisions that angered or pleased loved ones. Conventional wisdom said, "Be true to yourself, follow your path, and don't listen to naysayers." But that approach didn't grasp the whole picture. There was a lot of chatter in the world about how to make a decision and stick to it, but that was only half of the conversation. How did one live with the consequences and sacrifices of the decision?

In order to marry Josh, Holly was giving up everything she'd worked toward for the last decade. How was that fair? Years ago, despite caring about Josh, Holly had decided never to date. Last year about this same time, Ivy was the one who talked her into opening that door and courting Josh, knowing the relationship would bring joy and contentment unlike anything else could. But Ivy hadn't understood the sacrifices Holly might need to make if she fell in love.

The one thing Ivy did know is Holly

didn't regret her decision to lower her guard and allow herself to fall in love with Josh.

"Ivy?" Mamm called.

She turned to see her Mamm scurrying toward her.

"Hey." Mamm was breathless as she put her arm around Ivy's shoulders. "I . . . I need to tell you something." They walked slowly, Mamm's head down. "While making kettle corn and passing it out, I realized something."

Ivy waited, hoping Mamm's display of acceptance and kindness toward her wouldn't end with the conversation.

"I've been dismissive and stubborn. You opened up to me, telling me who you are, and all I could see was who you weren't. Since the day you were born, I wanted you to be the person I thought was best for you — a faithful Amish woman. But who you are is a kind, caring, let's-share-love-through-a-fancy-event person, and maybe my real problem with that is not who you are but how it looks." Mamm stopped and faced her. "I love who you are, Ivy. You have a really good, faithful heart. I still think you could find ways to be the real you inside the Old Ways, but if you don't, I choose to respect that, to trust you."

Ivy pulled her Mamm into a tight hug.

"Denki."

Mamm held her. "I see you, sweetie, and although I have concerns and reservations about the path you're taking, I'm proud of you." Mamm grinned. "Apparently Englisch events have the power to open eyes."

Ivy grinned. "They do, don't they? But what changed your mind?"

"A few minutes ago several verses came to me with such force I almost staggered. God called Abram to leave his people and his father's household, and I realized that I can't decide for you what God is saying to you." Mamm kissed her cheek. "I gotta go. My heart swelled with understanding, and I abandoned Holly with the kettle corn to find you." Mamm hurried off, but she turned and waved.

Relief coursed through Ivy, and hope bubbled like clear spring water. Maybe her Mamm would be in a good place by the time Ivy left.

She kept walking, and the petting zoo came into sight. Arlan was kneeling next to a small boy who looked nervous about touching the large cow in front of him. The petting zoo was actually just a pen with some of her family's own animals, supplemented by a few of Joshua's friendliest chickens. Tegan's dad had used his truck and horse trailer to haul them to the field. Ivy had brought her gentlest horse, Maple, and Red was supervising the children's interactions with Maple. Also on scene was Nell, the goat, Polka Dot, the cow, and her new baby, Bubbles.

When Tegan came up with the petting-zoo idea, Ivy knew she had to bring the sweet eight-week-old calf and Arlan, the "cow whisperer," to supervise.

"There, see?" Arlan said softly. "She's big compared to you, but she's just a baby and gentle as they come. Good girl, Bubbles." Arlan guided the child's hand onto the calf's side. Polka Dot stood next to her baby and munched her hay without reacting.

Ivy couldn't help but smile.

"Yeah," the boy whispered before pointing at a fluffy orange Silkie chicken. He grinned at Arlan and hurried to his parents and pulled them toward the chicken. Arlan was still crouched, chuckling as the boy and his folks scurried off.

"Having fun?" Ivy stepped forward and patted the calf's side.

Arlan's brows went up, and she knew he hadn't realized she was standing there.

He stood. "Actually, ya. When you said 'Englischer party,' this wasn't what I imagined. Other than their clothes, the decorations, and a few other small things, this really isn't that different from one of our big family gatherings."

Ivy stroked the calf's soft black-and-white coat. Arlan must've washed and brushed both cows before this event. "People are just people pretty much wherever you go. You have the good and the bad, but I only do family-friendly parties — ones like this or birthday parties or costume parties but mostly baby and bridal showers. Do you see something wrong with any of that?" Why did she want his opinion?

"Nee. I don't."

Wow, what a change from his previous viewpoint. His eyes met hers, and her heart leaped in her chest. What was wrong with her? Arlan had been different in the two months since Lorraine visited the farm. She knew it hadn't gone well, and he spoke less and less about the differences between Swartzentruber life and the Zook farm. When not working, he devoured books and wrote in journals.

His lips formed a charming smile as he petted the calf. "No need to look so shocked. I like the way you see life, Ivy Zook."

Her heart threatened to pound out of her chest, and she was tempted to put her hand over his. She shouldn't be interested in him. He wasn't staying, and neither was she. Her effort to open his heart to being less judgmental of Old Order people and Englischers hadn't been to persuade him to be a part of either group but rather to help him enjoy his life more when he returned to his Swartzentruber community.

Her face warmed as he held her gaze, and she broke eye contact. "So, um, speaking of enjoying life, have you ever gone caroling?"

A family walked up, and Arlan turned to greet them.

Ivy was sure that Mamm had volunteered her to lead the caroling again this year as part of a plan to convince Ivy she didn't want to leave the Amish. Mamm was a thinker, and Ivy found it hard to accept never again enjoying caroling practice or going caroling with her Amish friends. It was even harder to imagine never enjoying camaraderie with them again. She might see them on occasion, bump into them when shopping or such, but there would be a wall separating her from all those she'd grown up with. By next year she'd be Englisch, and there'd be no more Amish youth caroling, no more bonfires or frozen-pond gatherings. No more —

"Caroling?" Arlan asked.

The family was gone, and Arlan had returned to their previous conversation.

Ivy tried to focus. "It's where your youth group sings Christmas songs, sometimes while visiting people door-to-door and sometimes at a bonfire. You know, spreading Christmas cheer and all that?"

He looked confused. "I know about caroling from reading books set a hundred or two hundred years ago, but this is a current thing? And it's also among the Amish?"

"It is. My guess is Swartzentrubers aren't big on Christmas cheer."

He shrugged. "Some youth groups might do that. But my district is so tiny and shrinking constantly as families continue to move to the New York community. So, no, I'm afraid I've never spread Christmas cheer."

"Well, there's a first time for everything, Mr. Grinch."

He poked his hand under his straw hat and scratched his head. "Mr. who?"

"It's from a children's book."

"Are you holding out on what books you share, Ivy?"

Seeing his smile felt like warm sunshine after a cold rain.

"Maybe you're afraid of the frustration I'll

cause as we discuss characters and story lines."

He enjoyed teasing. She'd figured out that much.

She chuckled. "Ya, that's it. I'm afraid of the conversation we'd have about it." She liked their banter about books. They talked about them every mealtime, and their opposing views had caused boisterous chats and laughter but not a bit of frustration. "I don't own a copy. I read it at Tegan's years ago. Anyway, my point is that my Mamm is hosting caroling practice for the youth each week starting tomorrow." Ivy suppressed a grin as she moved to Polka Dot and rubbed the cow's side. "Actually, you don't have a choice in coming, and neither do I. Mamm volunteered me, without my permission, to direct the caroling since I've done it for our district the past five years, and she offered to host the gathering each week right under *your* room in the carriage house, in what's currently the storage area. So later today we'll clean out the bottom floor of the carriage house and set up chairs."

"Today?" He motioned at the livestock and temporary fencing. "And there will be a herd of cows waiting to be milked by the time we're back home."

"There's been no time to do it before now,

and we can't do it tomorrow since it's a Sabbath." She patted his shoulder. "You'll be fine. A little hard work never hurt anyone."

"*That* from a woman who wants to do nothing but plan parties for a living." He angled his head as his brows flitted up and down. Was he flirting with her?

She wagged her finger at him. "And you think that's easy?" Why was she flirting back?

He looked around at the tents, temporary fences, food, games, and livestock. "Apparently not."

"Tomorrow after the caroling the group will take off for the home of whoever is hosting the youth singing and snacks for the week. They'll be gone just in time for the evening milking to begin."

He narrowed his eyes, amusement dancing in them. "Are you trying to increase my workload, Ivy Zook?"

"Says the man who tripled the Zook herd."

A couple of children stopped several feet from Bubbles, and Arlan crouched again, smiling. "It's smart to be cautious around animals, but this one is gentle. It's okay." He motioned. "Kumm."

The boy and girl eased forward, and Ar-

Ian petted the cow, showing them it was okay and waiting patiently as each wavered on whether to touch the animal.

The list of everything Ivy would never get to do again once she left the Amish played over and over in her mind, screaming at her. A new thought hit. The list included something she hadn't thought of — no more talking to Arlan.

Hurt pierced her. Why did the list suddenly bother her so much? Was Mamm's plan, the one to open her eyes, working?

Or was the man patiently speaking to several children clouding her vision?

Seventeen

The sun hung low on the horizon as Arlan released twenty-four cows from the milking parlor into the pasture. The Zook farm had twenty-eight cows these days, but four were out of milking rotation for now, two were close to dropping a calf, and two were nursing calves.

His breath was frosty as he went outside the barn to refill the manmade watering hole. The air smelled a bit like snow, but it would be rare even to get flurries in mid-November.

A cow nudged him, and he turned. Cutie Pie wanted attention, and he patted her. He liked it here, although he was riddled with guilt day and night for feeling that way. He and Magda had been going to Sunday meetings, and he got a lot out of the messages, but there were still laws in the Word that these people didn't keep. Were they right? If so, how could that be when the Word was clear about it?

He returned to the barn, grabbed a pitchfork, and made quick work of mucking out stalls while Red hosed the concrete walkways between the line of stalls.

When the Zooks' relatives had brought cows from their farms, it'd been a really good day. Something about Red and him bringing this farm back to a respectable state felt right. They had most of the original stalls repaired. They'd also purchased two dozen more milkers, and they'd mowed, baled, and stored the hay for the season. Next on the list had been cleaning, oiling, and putting away the horse-drawn plows and mowers. It was done too, but the work harnesses still needed cleaning.

Ivy was right. Life had plenty of work and stress without hauling and heating water or milking every cow by hand. He enjoyed this kind of work, and he saw the benefit of allowing generators to help, but what did God really think about this way of living?

He'd received a letter from his older brother, Nathaniel. When he first saw it, he thought his brother might have sent a check, returning Arlan's investment in the New York farm. Instead, his brother had talked to their Daed, and Nathaniel assured Arlan that he simply needed to return home, with or without Magda, repent, and be faithful to Daed's community for a year. Then he could move to New York and help work the farm he had financially invested in. It was a huge relief to know he could still return home and even be a part of the farm he'd invested in years ago.

Laughter caught Arlan's attention. He looked through the open double-wide doors. Ivy and Magda were in the side yard with heavy sweaters on, and they'd set up several bales of hay with a target on them. His heart filled with warmth and light. His sister had found forgiveness and peace with the help of the Zooks, their Old Order bishop, and the church.

Ivy's feet moved swiftly while she laughed, as if her enthusiasm caused her to do a little dance. When she pulled back the arrow and let it go, it landed nowhere near the target.

He chuckled before turning back to his work.

Red turned off the hose and looked out the doors, probably to see what had Arlan's attention. "I got this. Go."

"Nee. I'm fine."

"You milked the herd by yourself last night for me." Red removed the milkers from the main line. "Evidently the girls are off for a bit, and at least one of them has your attention. Go."

Arlan frowned. "I should stay here. Your sister will appreciate it. Plus, she's confusing."

Red chuckled. "Ivy's an independent thinker, for sure, but she's also very kind and caring, so she confuses lots of Amish. But you know what's most likely to clear the confusion? Talking to the person."

Arlan dumped straw and dung onto the pile in the wheelbarrow. "Your family can't think it's a good idea for Ivy and me to get along."

"Wrong." Red laughed. "What are you possibly going to say or do that would cause an issue with us? Although, fair warning, it could be a problem for Ivy. She's planning to leave after Holly's wedding to live Englisch."

Arlan didn't look up from his work.

"This isn't new information to you, is it?"

"Nee." Arlan moved the wheelbarrow a few feet down the line.

"Then by all means talk to her, argue with her, flirt with her, and make her rethink leaving. Anything. Something. But don't stand there and do nothing." Red pointed toward the target area. *"Geh."*

Nervousness skittered through Arlan. Although most days they sat at the same kitchen table for at least two meals and had lively discussions about books, and although they'd worked the fall festival and cleaned out the carriage house together, he generally avoided her. "Okay, I'll go."

Maybe he could talk some sense into her about leaving. He hung the pitchfork on the wall of the barn, turned on the hose to rinse off his boots and hands, and strode toward the target area.

Ivy had yet to hit the target or the wall of hay bales that extended way beyond the target. How was that possible?

Magda cackled. "Try opening your eyes this time."

"Where's the fun in that?" Ivy asked.

Who aimed at a target and then shot with her eyes closed? Target practice only made sense if one was trying to learn or improve a skill. Otherwise she was wasting time.

Magda stood, her hands on her protruding stomach. "I have to go before I pee on my dress." She walked away, smiling and looking at the ground. She came within a few feet of Arlan and gasped. "Goodness, let a girl know you're nearby."

"Hey, Magda." Arlan shoved his hands into his jacket pockets. "I'm nearby."

"Denki." She giggled and kept walking.

The sky was purple and peach now, looking as if God were painting the sunset right this minute.

Ivy gathered a couple of arrows. "You any good at this?"

"Not particularly, but I think I could be horrible and still be better than you." He raised his brows, surprised by how amused he was at her, despite her wasting time on this game.

"Ya? Think so?" She smiled and held out the bow and arrow. "Have at it."

He took them, notched an arrow into the bowstring, pulled back, aimed, and released. The arrow hit the outer blue ring and sank in the hay bales.

"Not bad." Ivy got an arrow from the quiver, notched it, aimed, and let it fly. Her arrow hit a good two inches closer to the bull's-eye than his had.

"Wow. I'm impressed."

"Ya, me too." Ivy stared at the target. "The real trick is to do it with your eyes closed."

He picked up the quiver from the ground and pulled out an arrow. "It's a waste of time to shoot at a target with your eyes closed."

"And you need to save every minute" — Ivy poked his shoulder with her finger — "so you have more time to ponder right and wrong."

"True. There's a lot to think about because life outside the Swartzentruber community is quite confusing." Reading books and writing down his thoughts helped, but confusion over right and wrong was his constant companion.

"And life inside your Swartzentruber community wasn't?"

He hadn't thought of that. "Ya, actually it was. Very." There was a rule for everything, and it corresponded to a Bible verse, so the order made sense. But his Daed and Mamm seemed so caught up in keeping the rules that they were exhausted and wound tight and only saw their children through the eyes of what they hadn't done right. "Maybe I'm just the kind of person who feels vexed and confused no matter where I am."

"Maybe." She walked toward the target, gathering arrows. "Truth is, I constantly ponder what's right and wrong too." She plucked the last arrow from the ground. "It's hard on us to be obedient when an authority shoves information at us that differs from what we think is right."

"Wait. You see yourself as obedient?" He passed her an arrow.

She laughed. "Clearly you don't. But, ya, I think it's my nature to be obedient to Mamm and the Ordnung. Then I start thinking about what was said, and I can't be obedient because what's being said doesn't add up."

"Example, please."

They walked back to the firing point, and Ivy notched an arrow. "As I read it, the Word says that my long hair is my glory, and it is given as my covering, and yet I have to part it in the middle, comb it down tight, and pin it up in an exact bun in an exact spot on my head."

"What difference does it make how you wear your hair?"

"If it doesn't matter, why is wearing it any other way strictly forbidden?" She released the arrow, and it hit the yellow part of the target.

"Because we dress modestly, men and women."

"As far as hair goes, a ponytail or a messy bun would be modest, but those are forbidden."

"Ya, I see what you mean." He wasn't very good at debating why she should stay.

"Oh." She reached into her hidden pocket. "I picked up the mail earlier, and I forgot to shove yours under your door." She passed him a letter.

It was from Lorraine. "I don't know why she is still writing me."

"I imagine that's hard, but with a bit of time, surely she'll see your heart and sacrifice concerning Magda, and she'll love you for it and forgive you for leaving."

In each letter Lorraine wrote that she still wanted to marry him. Why?

He tapped an arrow against his pant leg. "It's not like that. I . . . I realized I wasn't in love with her. I just didn't know that until she came here."

"Does she know this?" Ivy held the bow out to him.

"Ya. I told her." He took the bow and notched an arrow. "The hard part is letting everyone down."

"Ya. I understand that far more than I want to. Most of us want to do what's expected of us and what we're told."

He released the arrow, hitting just outside Ivy's last arrow. "What do you think my chances are of the inner turmoil and confusion stopping?"

"I wouldn't know, but having faith in God's grace made a huge difference for me."

"What is grace to you, Ivy?"

"It's a gift." She lowered the bow and arrow. "I can't keep enough laws to earn my way into righteousness. I can, however, please Him through walking in faith, hope, and love."

Her words clicked inside him, as if unlocking something. Thoughts poured out from their formerly locked space, releasing equal parts optimism and confusion. He felt something similar when reading, except this wasn't just new worlds or ideas. These thoughts were feeding and changing his faith.

He couldn't manage to sort through them yet, but he knew his main concern. "Without rules people get lazy, and we'd end up a mess of self-indulgence."

"Maybe you're right. Seriously. But if being filled with faith, hope, and love isn't enough to guide us, how would something as lifeless as rules and laws manage it?" She aimed the arrow again, and this time she released it. It flew through the air and landed at the outer edge of the bull's-eye.

"But people's expectations hold us accountable."

"They sure do." She lowered the bow, fidgeting with it. "We just have to be sure that we're not so busy meeting their expectations that we forget God's expectations may look very different."

Did that mean God's expectations might look rebellious to well-meaning, good folk?

The new ideas and understandings crashed into him, shattering misconceptions like plate glass. No law caused him to leave home with Magda, and that was the hardest and best decision he'd ever made. "He's not asking people to follow a set of laws, is He?" Arlan paused, reeling at the depth of insight spinning in his head that went way beyond any words he could form. "He's saying, 'Follow Me.' "

Ivy nodded, but her face had become solemn. "I think so too, but how can we know we're following Him and not ourselves? I look at my sister, at all she's sacrificing to marry Josh, and I look at you, at all you sacrificed to get Magda to safety and to stay by her side. And whether you agree or not, my leaving is a sacrifice too. But how do any of us know if we're sacrificing the right things?"

"I see what you mean. If we'd chosen differently, we would've still sacrificed things, just different things."

"Ya, exactly. Is my sister right to sacrifice so much to marry the man she loves?"

"When I was debating whether to leave with Magda, I imagined what the outcome might be if I left with her, and then I imagined the possible outcome if I didn't leave. Were the ends going to justify the means?"

"Then it sounds as if love justifies the

sacrifice." Ivy tapped an arrow against her shoulder. "The health needs of the Amish can be met in other ways, but only Holly and Josh can fill up to overflowing the love between them, and only they can have their children. Everything else is a sacrifice worth making." Ivy pointed the arrow at him. "That about the ends justifying the means was *really* good, Arlan. I get it." She shivered. "But I'm cold, and it's getting late."

"Okay." He took the bow and arrow from her. "I think I'll try some target practice in the dark. Can't be any worse than you with your eyes closed."

She pushed the rods of two arrows against his chest. "This is true. Enjoy." She scurried toward the house.

Arlan looked skyward, seeing twinkling stars. It seemed as if God was saying, *Hear Me. Think. Trust your heart to Me, not to any group of people.*

Years ago while working in a field one day, he'd said a prayer in which he had repented and accepted Christ. In that moment his trust in grace had seemed invincible. But his mind, Daed, and preachers kept telling him to fulfill the laws of God, and he fell back into those ways.

Tonight the sky had more stars than he could count, and in his mind's eye they seemed to represent people. Did God guide and lead all those people with a singular church's belief of how life should be lived?

He aimed an arrow in the direction of the target although it was now too dark to see it. But this is what it felt like to try to understand God — like shooting an arrow in the dark.

By grace you are saved.

And he knew that hitting the bull's-eye of understanding God saved no one. And he was pretty sure no one really hit that bull's-eye no matter how much they claimed to. God was too vast for laws to be sufficient in pleasing Him, too holy for any amount of law keeping to come close to being good enough.

Grace was the answer, and grace freed him from the need to follow Old Testament laws or to be exacting.

So did that mean he didn't need to follow the Old Order Amish ways either? He'd come out here to talk Ivy out of leaving, and *this* was the question on his mind?

EIGHTEEN

Ivy stood in front of her caroling group, taking in the sight of the carriage house filled to capacity with her friends' singing and their smiling faces. They had a fire going in the potbellied wood stove, an addition Mamm had made to the space years ago to accommodate such gatherings and stave off the mid-November chill. With that and the warmth from all her friends, the small space was cozy. She tried not to cringe as several male singers hit some sour notes in the chorus of "Angels We Have Heard on High." Arlan stood near the area where the sour notes originated, but in three weeks of caroling practice, she'd realized he had a great singing voice.

Some of the new singers the group had gained this year were fantastic, like Magda and Arlan. Others not so much. But it really didn't matter. Judging by the laughter and smiles at each rehearsal, the whole group enjoyed the practices. It was nice that Magda had been allowed to participate, especially since she couldn't attend the youth singings. Those were for finding a spouse, and as understanding as Ivy's people had been about Magda, they wouldn't be comfortable with her attending that.

Someone snickered as the song ended. Ah, they were messing with her. Ivy narrowed her eyes at the group of guys sitting in the area of the wrong notes. "*Lovely* harmonies, Snow Buntings. But it sounds to me as if a few of you are volunteering to sing a solo." The snickering stopped. "No one? Fine. Moving on."

How Ivy adored Christmas and everything about the season. The beautiful carols, the cozy feel, the decorations in the pharmacy, the food, and most of all the story of her Savior being born into such a lowly but loving family.

What should they sing now? She flipped to the next page of the lyrics. "Turn your lyric sheets to 'Lo, How a Rose E'er Blooming.' Remember, we're trying to memorize as many words as we can over the next few weeks. Our first caroling takes place in just three weeks, which is mid-December."

"It's a lot of words," a male voice called. "We think you should hold up signs for us. Or at least some hand signals." More snickering.

Ivy held up a finger and shook it at them. "Nope and nope. Ready?" She started singing, and the group quickly joined her.

"Lo, how a Rose e'er blooming from tender stem hath sprung!"

This was such a beautiful song. As they sang the familiar lyrics, Ivy found herself looking at Magda, who was reading her lyric sheet. At the first practice she said she'd never sung these songs before. Ivy wasn't sure how much actual caroling Magda would be able to do. She'd have a baby right around the time everyone celebrated the birth of the Savior. From the little that Magda had told her about the situation, the baby's Englischer father didn't want anything to do with her or the child. He wanted freedom. But the price would be that he'd miss everything. And Magda was wonderful. Her baby was sure to be an incredible blessing to all those around her.

"It came, a floweret bright, amid the cold of winter, when half spent was the night."

Listen, Ivy, a voice seemed to say to her as the song flowed through her throat and lips. She sang the rest of the words on autopilot, letting the words resound in her heart.

"Amid the cold of winter." A "tender stem" that was Jesus bloomed.

What was God trying to tell her?

The song ended. Chills ran across her skin, from her head to her feet, and her heart seemed to be doing a dance of some sort. She needed to stop the rehearsal to figure this out. It was almost time to disperse for the Sunday singing and games anyway. "Okay, Snow Buntings. That sounded so good that I think we should stop the rehearsal."

"You sure? Maybe we should sing it again to see if sounding good was a mistake," Lizzie, one of Ivy's friends from childhood, teased. Ivy had said that same line many times in her rehearsals.

What would Ivy gain by becoming Englisch that would be worth giving up her Amish family, both her immediate family and the extended "family" of the community? In light of all Holly was sacrificing, this question wasn't new for Ivy, but it felt different tonight — as if God was trying to talk to her. She needed to get somewhere quiet.

"Nee, get out of here." She waved her hand to shoo them away. How she loved this group. "Please stack your lyric sheets in the crate by the door. See you again next week. It's just a few Sundays till Christmas."

Magda and Arlan hesitated, neither falling in line to leave nor approaching Ivy. She smiled at them. "You're free too. Geh." She waved goodbye to her group.

Everyone left, and soon she heard heavy footfalls on the steps leading to the apartment above the carriage house.

She grabbed her black sweater hanging over the back of her stool and looked out the window. Daylight saving time had ended earlier in the month, so at six o'clock it was already dark. Still, she could see well enough to know some of the singers were in groups, chatting rather than quickly getting into their rigs. The desire to get alone somewhere and pray pressed in on her.

Could she sneak off before someone tried to talk to her? As she stepped outside, the cold wind hit her, and she tightened the sweater around her. Going to think somewhere outside in the wind wouldn't do.

An idea struck. She crossed the dark yard and headed into the barn. Once inside she picked up a kerosene lantern that was hanging on the wall and lit it. The ladder to the hayloft was no longer broken, one of Arlan's many repairs on the farm. With the lantern in one hand, she made sure of each step as she climbed the ladder. When she reached the loft, she walked around the piles of hay until she saw what she was looking for.

There they were. In the very back of the hayloft, she'd stashed a few sealed shoebox-size plastic containers. She knelt, set the lantern on one of the plastic bins, and opened another. Inside was her secret stash of Christmas decorations, the ones she didn't dare put in the front of the pharmacy for fear of their getting broken. Every year she found a few old ornaments in yard sales and added them to her stash. If Mamm had noticed them, she'd never said anything.

She unwrapped a couple of glass ornaments and watched them twinkle in the lamplight before setting them in the hay. The one she was searching for was somewhere in this section. *There.* She felt the silky cloth that shrouded it: a circular blown-glass ornament with each side shaped like a rosebud and frosted with glittery "snow."

She unwrapped the ornament and touched its contrasting smooth and rough surfaces, a red rose with white snow. A flower blooming in midwinter. Was the client who gave her the ornament the person who had told Ivy she should focus on blooming where she was planted? Ivy didn't like that saying because it felt like a cop-out, a reason not to try to improve one's situation, a reason not to fight for who one really was. Just because someone was born on a farm didn't mean she shouldn't live and work in a big city or live in an Englisch historic home and plan parties. But maybe —

"Hallo? Is someone up there? I see light."

Arlan. She wouldn't mind talking to him about this, but she was drawn to him, so his presence only muddied the water.

"Ya, it's me, Ivy." Maybe he'd go back to whatever he was doing.

He was climbing the ladder. "You ended practice real quick. Is something wrong?"

She hesitated, but the truth was, she needed to talk to him. "No. And yes." She looked at the ornament in her hands. "I don't know."

"Apparently we each hid items in the haymow on our farms." Arlan crossed over to her.

When he'd told her nearly three months' back that he used to hide his books, it hadn't surprised her. They were alike in many ways.

He knelt next to her. "What's this?"

Ivy handed him the rose ornament. "My

234

forbidden stash of Christmas decorations."

"It reminds me of some of the words in the song we just sang." He turned it over in his hand.

"Ya. One of the clients I cleaned for gave it to me a few years ago after I admired it. She said she'd bought the ornament on a trip to Switzerland many years ago and since my ancestors were Swiss, I should have it. I didn't dare tell the sweet woman that the Amish don't allow any Christmas decorations at home."

"But you're getting to enjoy it now." He handed the glass rose back to her.

She took it and held it up by its string to twirl in the lamplight so that the snow glittered. "Guess I am. No judgments about it?"

He shook his head, and a corner of his mouth turned upward. "I'm done with that."

Nice, and he seemed so much more at peace. Where was her peace?

He pointed at the ornament. "So the rose is Christ."

"Ya. And the winter is how dark the world was before He was born into such a humble circumstance."

"It is for freedom that Christ set us free."

Her eyes met his. "Amen."

Suddenly she knew what was really bothering her. Freedom in Christ was enough. She could be her true self *and* bloom here with the precious love of her family and community. It wasn't perfect, but it was hardly the rough beginnings that Christ had. What could the world offer her that was more fulfilling than what she already had? If she lived Englisch, she would be free to be her real self but only in some ways. In other ways she'd be giving up her ability to be all of her real self. "After Daed died, I boxed up a lot of things and shoved them into the back of my closet, trying not to feel the hurt of all we'd lost. But in doing that I also boxed up parts of who I am. Then I started believing this Amish life isn't who I am, but it is — at least more of who I am than I realized."

Questions flooded her.

Was love about sacrificing part of who a person really was in order to give to those he or she loved? Isn't that what Christ did when He came to earth? Where would any of us be if He hadn't sacrificed part of who He was?

Would leaving the Amish cause her to have stronger bonds with Christ, with others, and with herself by the end of her life?

Would an Englisch life put her more in

touch with who God created her to be?

She didn't know what she'd do instead of party planning if she chose to stay. That career wasn't the point. It never had been. What she longed for, what she sought after, was full authenticity with herself and who God created her to be. The rest would eventually fall into place — whether it was event planning or something she couldn't yet imagine.

NINETEEN

Arlan stood on the porch of his childhood home, studying his parents. The mid-December wind cut through his coat as if it didn't exist. His driver had the car running, staying warm while he waited for Arlan.

He'd known this visit would be difficult, but he'd expected to be allowed inside and to be able to talk to his family for a while. Instead, his Daed stood his ground, refusing to let Arlan go inside, and so far his Daed wasn't hearing anything he had to say. Magda hadn't come, unwilling to hear Daed's hurtful words or to watch Mamm struggle with his harsh decrees. She also feared that, despite all else, they would try to make her stay.

Arlan's hands were deep in his coat pockets, and he could feel the slips of paper he'd carefully printed information on. How would he get these to any of his siblings?

"You need to leave." His Daed's voice held

no mercy or understanding.

The pain in Arlan's chest grew worse by the minute. Who was this man looking back at him? The sense of betrayal and abandonment bore down on him. How did a man turn his back on his children so easily?

"Daed, I've worked beside you my entire life, helped maintain and make this place what it is, and because I've chosen a different Plain order, you'll disown me?"

"I have nothing else to say on the matter. You disobeyed me. You ran off with your sister, embarrassing your Mamm and me in front of everyone. God said to honor your parents. I hope you reap all you've sown."

"His Word also says, fathers, do not provoke your children to anger. It says to be kind and gentle and forbearing. Magda won't even set foot on this place for fear of what you'll say or do. Open your eyes, Daed."

"They are open, and I see you. You're manipulative and deceitful."

"Okay." Arlan sighed. "I'll leave. But I want you to know that we can have a good relationship despite what the church says. *You* have to decide whether I'm worthy to you as a human and a son or whether you'll let the church tell you who we'll be for the rest of our lives. Whatever you decide, know that I'm open to your reaching out at any point, even thirty years from now."

"Your life is open to rebellion and the world. That's what it's open to, so just leave me out of it." Daed went to the front door and clutched the handle.

Daed motioned for Mamm to follow him, but she stood firm. "Is Magda really okay?"

"Ya, Mamm. She is. God provided a perfect place for her, and she's doing well. She said to tell you that she loves both of you and that she misses you, Mamm. But trust is broken, and she won't come here until she feels safe and respected."

"She wants respect?" Daed's voice boomed. "For what? What has she done that deserves respect?"

"She's not asking you to think highly of her. She's asking you to respect that she's a sinner the same as you, and she's asking you to respect God's grace toward her. That's all, Daed — respect God's grace toward her."

"It's my job as a parent to hold my children accountable," Daed said.

"You hold your children accountable every working minute of every day for not being perfect, but God doesn't ask that. He said, "Come unto me, all ye that labour and are heavy laden, and I will give you rest.

Take my yoke upon you, and learn of me; for I am meek and lowly in heart: and ye shall find rest unto your souls." Arlan drew a breath. "Rest unto our souls, Daed. Because legalism and perfectionism are heavy and exhausting."

"The Englisch are all about the mercy of God. You want to be like them, eh? You know so much, and you're full of yourself. Now go."

Mamm closed the gap and hugged him. *"Ich lieb du."* She held him tight.

"I love you too, Mamm. That won't change. Not ever."

Daed grabbed Mamm by the arm. "Go inside. Now."

Mamm opened the front door. *"Kinder.* Kumm."

His siblings rushed out, and Daed looked too shocked to respond. Arlan hugged them and told them he loved them, and he secretly passed the slips of paper to as many of them as he could. It had the phone numbers and addresses for the Zooks' farm and Greene's Pharmacy as well as Jules's cell number. He couldn't take his siblings with him, but he could be sure the older ones had a way to call for help if they needed it.

His Daed clapped his hands. "Inside.

Everyone." He pointed at Arlan. "Get off my property."

Daed didn't seem to have noticed the pieces of paper. Arlan waved to his brothers and sisters as he descended the steps and got into the car. It was hard to breathe. Harder still to keep tears from forming.

The driver said nothing, and the car easily covered mile after mile of narrow back roads. Even though the trip from his home to the Zook farm didn't take very long by vehicle, he couldn't wait to get out of the car and get to his room above the carriage house. He needed time alone, maybe weeks of it, as his emotions churned like clouds on a stormy day.

Too many thoughts assaulted him and scattered before he could focus on just one. Hurt, anger, and grief threatened to suffocate him. How would he live with himself, knowing he'd left his siblings behind? But how could he go back there to live? He'd burned that bridge.

The driver remained silent as he went up the long gravel driveway to the Zook farm and pulled in behind another car that was in front of the Zook home. Arlan paid the driver and got out.

Ivy was getting out of the other vehicle. Where was her coat? Their eyes locked, and he knew she was struggling too.

He took off his coat, walked to her, and put it around her shoulders.

She gazed up, her blue eyes brimming with tears. "I told Tegan and the landlady that I'm not leaving the Amish."

The news stabbed a knife into his heart and yet also elated him, and he couldn't stop himself from wrapping his arms around her.

She shuddered. "I feel sick about talking Clara into accepting me as a tenant and then going back on my word."

They were both trembling.

A few tears escaped and ran down his face. "I told my Daed that Magda and I are not returning."

She drew a shaky breath and held him. "What are we doing?" Ivy whispered.

"I don't know. I really don't."

TWENTY

Holly studied the handsome man as they knelt in front of each other. His eyes held kindness, shining bright in the flickering candlelight. His hand was warm on hers. Was this a dream? She never, ever wanted to forget one detail of their wedding day.

The Zook house was lit by dozens of evergreen-scented candles. This twentieth day of December was gray and snowy. But inside her home that was packed with hundreds of Amish and a few Englischers from Greene's, Holly couldn't imagine anything more vibrant and warm. How long they'd yearned for this moment, their hands together in front of Holly's bishop, their wedding vows said, and the closing prayer still echoing in her mind.

Benuel finished the prayer. Josh and she rose and faced the gathering of their beloved friends and family. The bridal party — their side sitters — beamed at them, some wiping tears of joy. Holly spotted Magda on one of the benches. She was grimacing.

Labor pains.

Before sunrise this morning Magda had come to Holly and let her know that she was having painful contractions. But Magda wanted to see the wedding if she could. Even though Esther, the Amish midwife, had been invited to the wedding as a friend, Holly called her to verify she was coming today. Esther had arrived early to check on Magda's progress.

The plan was for Magda to go to the room above the carriage house when her labor pains became more intense. There she would have privacy from the many visitors who would be in this home until sundown. Judging by Magda's face, Holly was sure she would head there soon.

Holly and Joshua were ushered into the parlor, and the next half hour was filled by chatting with some of the guests while family and friends in the next room rearranged the rows of benches, turning some into tables and using the others as seats. Josh and Holly didn't have to help with the work for the rest of today, and the festivities would go on until after sundown. But tomorrow they'd make up for it — waking before dawn to start washing the tablecloths and napkins, bringing furniture back into the house and putting it in place, and taking care of the gazillion other things people had to do after hosting hundreds of people for a wedding and two meals.

Holly spotted Jules, Lyle, and Brandon working their way through the throng of Amish people toward her and Josh. Every room in the house was bursting with people. How many Amish were in the barn, staying warm and out of the way until their time to eat?

"Holly." Jules had her arms out as she approached. "Congratulations." Holly pulled Jules into a tight hug.

Lyle winked at Holly as Jules released the embrace. "We're thrilled for you, kiddo."

Brandon grinned. "My Amish little sister, all grown up and married."

Josh put his hand on Holly's arm, grinning. "Thank you all for everything you've done for her. I'm so sorry she can't continue working for Greene's."

Lyle gave a slow nod. "We understand." He leaned in closer. "Just so you know, Holly Noelle, you'll always have a place at Greene's if your new bishop ever changes his mind."

Jules glanced at a text on her phone. "I'm sorry to have to leave, but there're some problems at the clinic and my team needs help. You'll call me later to update me on Magda, right?"

"I will." Holly hugged Jules.

Lyle shifted from one foot to the other. "We all rode together, so we need to go too, plus" — he pointed out the window — "it's snowing again, and the weather report says there's quite a bit of snow on the way. The roads will be okay for buggies, I think."

"Ya, horses and buggies are much better equipped for winter travel. Besides that, the Amish guests can make themselves a pallet and stay overnight if it gets too bad. That's part of the reason we didn't mind having the wedding so late in December." She hugged Lyle and Brandon. "Thanks, everyone, for being here."

As they said their goodbyes, an aunt came into the parlor, smiling. "It's time." She held out her arm, and Josh took it. Her aunt was honored with seating the bride and groom at their table today, and then she would return for the other side sitters, each one entering the room in a set order.

The long table, which was big enough for the bride and groom and their side sitters, was covered in a crisp white cloth with blue trim. Josh was seated at the head of the table, and Holly was to his left. Next to her was Ivy, and next to Josh was Arlan, because all side sitters had to be single. Besides, Josh and Arlan had become close.

Bishop Benuel was hoping Arlan would join their Old Order church and thought that Arlan being at the bride-and-groom table would help him feel like a part of the community. Holly would pair him with Ivy in the wedding games as the day proceeded. There was definitely a spark between the two of them, and Holly wanted to nurture it.

The sound of glass breaking echoed through the room, and Holly started to get up, but Josh put his hand over hers. "You've done enough for today." He winked.

Holly relaxed, glad for time off her feet. The wedding preparations had been a huge undertaking that included moving most of the furniture out of the house and into the carriage house yesterday, cooking for the past several days and finishing a dozen tasks, like sewing and cleaning. Today had begun at three in the morning with milking cows, fixing breakfast, and finishing up preparation of the house and food for about four hundred guests.

Women set large platters of food on their table — a bounteous feast of roasted chicken, mashed potatoes, cooked celery, bowls of fruit, platters of cheese, and homemade bread.

With each bite Holly tasted the love from a community of married women — aunts, cousins, and church members — who'd cooked today's feast. Guests ate in rounds, and while a few tables were still being served, one of Josh's side sitters began singing. Everyone around the wedding table joined in first, and then others added their voices.

She and Josh soon cut their beautiful wedding cake, and the women servers also sliced or dipped other desserts and filled mugs with coffee or hot chocolate. The single men at the wedding table began singing various songs, and everyone joined in. Then Ivy and Arlan got the wedding games started. They played a lot of guessing games, some while blindfolded. Laughter filled the house, and Holly's cheeks hurt from nonstop grinning. The carolers stood in front of the large window in the parlor next to the roaring fire and sang while the snow came down in huge flakes.

Holly's heart soared as she and Josh sat on the couch, watching and listening, and it seemed she had hardly blinked before the guests were leaving. More than half of the people had said their goodbyes before the evening meal, as was the tradition. This was a time for more intimate friendships and relatives. Her aunts served heated leftovers, cold cuts, cheese, and more homemade bread, and, of course, church spread, the peanut butter concoction the Amish loved.

Winter's short day caught her off guard. It was dark now. The midwife, Esther, had come in from the carriage house several times throughout the day to update Holly on how Magda was doing. But the last time she had updated Holly was more than two hours ago, when she'd said that Magda was doing well and was almost at the pushing phase of labor.

Holly moved to the window and looked toward the carriage house. The white, snowy landscape of the Zook farm looked peaceful and clean. Beautiful. Huge flakes were still coming down from the dark, cloudy sky. How many inches had fallen already?

Mamm came to her side and put an arm around her shoulders. "A Christmastime baby is meant to be on our farm, ya?" She must've noticed that Holly was staring at the carriage house.

"Seems so, doesn't it? You delivered each of your three babies at Christmastime. Should we go to the carriage house? Just to check on Magda?"

Mamm nodded, a tender smile glowing on her face. "Ya."

As they walked toward the back door to grab their coats, Josh's bishop, Stephan, came toward them with his wife at his side.

"Denki for everything, Betty, Holly. It's been a day filled with God's glory, but it's time for us to go."

"Denki." Holly slid into her coat. "We're going to check on Magda, so we'll walk out with you." She peered through the glass on the back door, seeing a figure walking toward the farmhouse.

Holly opened the door, and Esther stepped inside. "Before anyone asks, it's a healthy boy. He's breathing well and is already nursing. My helper is sitting with Magda."

Esther paused, and Holly's heart skipped a beat. "Is everything okay?"

Esther glanced at the numerous guests beyond this small gathering at the back door. She leaned in. "I don't want to alarm anyone."

Holly's chest tightened. In the last few months, she'd had more than one nightmare about a teen delivering a baby during a snowstorm, and that had prompted her to talk to Jules and Lyle and Brandon about her concerns about Magda's labor and delivery.

"What's going on?" Stephan asked while putting on his coat, looking as if he was ready to dash to the phone shanty and call for an ambulance.

Esther pursed her lips. "Magda delivered the placenta about half an hour after the babe was born, but she's been bleeding more than I like to see. If it doesn't stop soon, we'll need to call an ambulance."

"With these road conditions I'm not sure an ambulance could get through, and if it does, a ride would be a risk for Magda and her new baby," Holly said. "I talked with Lyle, Brandon, and Jules a few weeks ago about what might happen at the birth and what we needed to have on hand in case something went wrong. We might need the ambulance, but before we call them, I have a medicine they recommended that I'd like to try."

The midwife looked at the bishop as if waiting for permission.

"Ya, of course." His eyes held concern. "Although this isn't my district, you do what needs to be done and waste no time." He seemed like a different man as he gestured for Holly to go. He turned to his wife.

She nodded and looped her arm through Mamm's. "How about we go mingle and do what we can to keep everyone distracted and thinking everything is just fine?"

Mamm nodded. "Ya. Good thinking."

When Holly turned to go after the needed items, Josh was there. She squeezed his hand before hurrying through the house, up the stairs, and to her room. She grabbed her prepared birth bag and opened it to double-check its contents. Inside was her stethoscope, blood pressure cuff, two large bottles of an electrolyte drink, a large plastic cup with a straw, nonprescription Tylenol and Motrin tablets, and a white prescription bag that held six tablets of Methergine, a medicine to stimulate the uterus to contract — and hopefully stop excess bleeding after childbirth without a trip to the hospital.

She slung the bag over her shoulder and flew down the stairs and out the door. Esther was going toward the carriage house, and Holly quickly caught up to her. Esther had been a young woman of twenty-eight when she delivered Holly. The two trudged across the snowy yard, and Holly glanced behind her, noticing a coatless Josh and his bishop following them.

Esther looked at the men behind her. "I've

set up a curtain to divide the room, and I've put chairs in place. Magda said any visitors are welcome to that area."

They went up the stairs to the carriage house and Holly hurried inside. "Magda?" Holly paused outside the curtain Esther had hung. "May I come in?"

"Ya, Holly. That's fine."

Joshua and Bishop Stephan took a seat outside the curtained-off area.

Holly entered Magda's half of the room. Esther's helper, an Amish girl named Rose, who was a few years younger than Holly, was in a chair near the window.

Magda looked up at Holly, radiant despite her slightly pale face and her mussed hair under her prayer Kapp. Her body was covered from the chest down in blankets, and her tiny newborn was wrapped in a swaddle and asleep in her arms. She grinned. "Holly, look at him. Last night I had a dream of God's hands touching my baby's chest with a blessing of gold before He placed this little one in my arms. And here he is."

Holly's eyes misted as she leaned in. "He's beautiful, Magda. Now I need you to take some medicine for me, okay? For your bleeding."

"Okay."

Holly opened her bag and quickly set up everything as Jules had taught her.

She motioned to Esther's helper. "Would you hold this cup for her, please." Rose did as Holly asked. Holly smiled, trying not to sound or look too businesslike. "Magda, I'd like you to drink as much of this as you can to replenish your body. You may have a few more pills to take, one every four hours." She looked up at the midwife. "Esther, I know you have a stopwatch in your supplies. Set it for ten minutes, then for thirty. Let's put fresh padding under her so we'll have an idea whether the bleeding has slowed in ten minutes. We'll do the same for the thirty-minute mark. The medicine will need an hour for full effect, but we should notice some improvement before then. Magda, you're likely to feel more afterbirth pains because of the medication, so let's give you some Tylenol."

Magda smiled, staring at her baby's sleeping face. "I don't mind the pain. He's worth it."

Holly gave Magda the two Tylenol tablets, and the helper held the drink. Lyle had said to give Magda Tylenol instead of Motrin if she was having more-than-normal bleeding. *Please, God, let these things I have for her be enough.* They could still call an ambulance, but what if the weather became worse?

Holly checked the new mother's blood pressure. Thank goodness the numbers were good. If Magda's blood pressure was dropping, they'd need to call an ambulance for sure. Holly listened to her heartbeat while assuring her of how wonderful she'd done and was doing, how beautiful her baby was, and how everything was fine. She could hear Josh and his bishop talking softly on the other side of the curtain.

Esther checked Magda at ten minutes, but she was unsure if the bleeding had slowed. That wasn't a good sign.

Holly sat beside Magda, encouraging her to continue sipping on the electrolyte solution as they oohed over the baby. Magda was a trooper. If the amount of liquid Holly was pushing had her queasy, she didn't mention it. She drank three cups as the minutes ticked by.

Esther stood from her chair in the corner. "It's been thirty minutes." The midwife walked to Magda's bed and lifted the blanket.

Holly couldn't see everything, but she saw the midwife slide a new pad under Magda and press on Magda's lower stomach.

"Gut, gut." Esther let out a sigh. "The

bleeding has slowed significantly."

Relief eased through Holly, relaxing her aching shoulders. Her prayers had been answered. "Let's give her at least one more dose in three and a half hours." She smiled at Magda. "I'll ask my husband to bring you some wedding food. Something with iron and protein would be perfect."

"Denki, Holly." Magda looked and sounded better too. The little one was nursing again. How great to see a healthy mother and baby.

Holly stepped around the curtain. "They're doing well."

Josh nodded. "Gut. And I heard what you wanted." He stood and moved in close. "I like the sound of you calling me 'husband.' Ya, wife?"

"Suits us already." She waved as he went down the stairs.

Bishop Stephan remained sitting, seeming reluctant to leave. "No ambulance needed?"

Holly shook her head. "Not today, thanks to God's mercy."

Stephan grimaced and nodded. "Let's go to the downstairs carriage house and finish talking about this."

"Okay." Holly put on her coat and stepped outside onto the landing. The wind blew powdery snow across the lawn. What did

Stephan need to say to her? Did he disapprove of something she had done to help Magda?

After they were on the ground, he opened the door to the downstairs part of the carriage house where they sometimes stored carriages and where Ivy held caroling practices.

He struck a match and lit a lantern. "It seems God used some sort of medicine to make a difference today for Magda."

Holly closed the door, blocking out the cold wind. "Ya. It's called Methergine."

"Why did you have to get it from your room? Why didn't Esther have it?"

"Esther is a fantastic midwife, but legally, because of her limited education and because she doesn't have the covering of a medical group, she can't get access to modern medicine for such situations. I'm sure she could get her hands on it, but if she was caught with it, she'd face serious legal trouble. But Julie, as Magda's health-care provider, prescribed the Methergine, Brandon filled it at Greene's, and I picked it up, which was perfectly legal."

He jammed his hands into his coat pockets. "Years ago when I was a teen and living in my parents' home, my older sister and her husband had their first child. I wasn't in the room, but I still remember my Mamm's panic when her bleeding didn't stop after the delivery. Mamm sent me to the phone shanty to call an ambulance." He drew a ragged breath. "But we lived far away from everything, so it took a really long time for the ambulance to reach us. My sister could've died that day. As it was, she came close. Too close, and she was weak for a couple of months." He stared at the wall for a moment. "If you had been in our community that day with your knowledge, you would've made sure my sister had the medicines she needed. Just like you've been doing for Joshua's Mamm with her diabetes. I can tell she's better since you've been instructing her about medicines and a healthy diet."

"Denki." Holly tried to follow what he was saying, but her mind and emotions had absorbed so much today his point seemed blurry. "She'll never be cured, but we can control it, and she could live to be ninety."

Was he just reminiscing? Maybe releasing pent-up concerns about Magda?

The bishop closed his eyes for a moment and then opened them again. "I'm sorry, Holly. I was blind to your value, but as I sat in that room upstairs, listening and praying, God opened my eyes. I want you to stay on your health-care mission. Our people can rely on you."

Was this real? Holly couldn't get her mouth to form words. She blinked back tears.

"You have to promise me, though, that your own babies and husband will always come first."

The door opened, and Josh stepped in. "I took Magda her food." He closed the door. "Everything okay?"

Her eyes locked on Josh's. "More than okay." As tired as her body was, her heart was overflowing with joy, and she smiled. "Bishop, my husband and babies will always come first. I promise they will."

TWENTY-ONE

The town twinkled with electric Christmas lights reflecting on the powdery snow as Arlan drove toward Greene's Pharmacy. It was closed and locked tight, as was every other store in downtown Raysburg on the evening of Christmas Day. But she and Arlan were just out and about to enjoy the night.

"You're in the middle of the road." Ivy laughed. "The town may be empty, but you should still pick a lane, Arlan."

"Why?" He chuckled as he steered the horse to one lane. "I was having fun."

"It's just the way things are done. Deal with it," she teased.

He brought the carriage to a stop in front of Greene's Pharmacy. While Arlan hitched the horse to a post, Ivy stepped up to Greene's storefront window. She touched the cold plate glass. It was smooth, completely free of scratches, and was even more beautiful than the previous glass. Some

261

snow flurries swirled around her as she stood admiring her many decorations.

She looked over her shoulder. "What do you think, Arlan? You haven't had a chance to see the full setup since things have been so busy at the farm."

Inside the pharmacy the blue spruce that Ivy had selected from a local grower was adorned with a wide red-and-white ribbon that wrapped the entire tree. Strands of white Christmas lights were tucked into the blue-green branches so that the tree emitted a twinkling glow, and they illuminated the many handmade ornaments, mostly gifts from Greene's patients.

Arlan studied the window. "I've never seen anything like it. It's beautiful."

A golden star glimmered from its top perch. Next to the tree an animatronic snowman held up a stick hand in a wave, although its movement was turned off while the store was closed. A handcrafted Nativity scene was positioned under a wood shelter. She and Red had made the figurines' shelter when they were teens. And one of Ivy's favorite additions to the decorations — a miniaturized scene of Raysburg with a few tiny horses and buggies and a replica of downtown, complete with Greene's — sat in a bed of puffy snow in the bay window.

More lights, tinsel, and faux snow touched every visible corner of the front part of the pharmacy.

She nibbled on her bottom lip. "I agree." She pointed at the Nativity scene that was front and center in the window. "Christmas means so much to me. God sent His Son for *us.* We should be celebrating every day, shouting it clearly like these decorations do from the window."

Arlan took one of her gloved hands into his. "I know."

Ivy's heartbeat sped up, and she squeezed his hand.

He drew a deep breath. "I have one more gift to share with you."

"What? The whole family exchanged gifts this morning. Why now?"

"Because I wanted us to be alone, and we're never alone on the farm."

"This is true, especially since you became an uncle five days ago."

He smiled. "On the day before Christmas Eve, I had a long talk with Benuel."

"The bishop." Her heart turned a flip. "Ya?" She liked this — standing here holding hands with him under the twinkling Christmas lights.

"I'm officially joining the Old Order church. I start instruction in the spring."

Wow. So he'd really followed through on this. "That's great, Arlan."

"And you're staying Amish for good?"

She nodded. "I am. And I'll go through instruction this spring too. It was difficult to let go of that *Englisch* dream, but I can't change the person I am on the inside, and that person is Amish. I once told Mamm I *was* tulle and lace and twinkly lights, and that is a part of me, but it's not who I am. Who I am can't be defined by breaking bonds with my family. It can only be defined by blooming right where He planted me."

"As true as that is for you, it's not true for me."

She tugged on his coat collar. "I'm grateful He directed each of us according to His wisdom."

Arlan gently squeezed her hand. "During my conversation with the bishop, we talked about this." He gave a nod at the store, and she knew he meant the decorations.

"You did?" She tried to catch his eye. She wasn't sure if that was good news or not.

Arlan smiled at her. "He sees your heart, Ivy. And so do I. You carry joy wherever you go, and you want to shine that joy into the world. That's why you love throwing parties. Benuel said he sees nothing wrong with you continuing that work under the right circumstances."

Ivy looked at a little sparrow ornament that she'd perched on a Christmas tree branch. "I think that bird has already flown away. Tegan was really disappointed in me about the apartment and about all the things I can't do that she can regarding the parties. She's gotten a full-time job and found a new roommate. She and Clara have forgiven me, but they're moving on without me." As wonderful as Tegan was when it came to running events, she couldn't do the main organizing. Her gifting was helper, not leader.

"But do you have to give up all of it just because you won't be Englisch?"

"The bookings have to be internet based. Without the internet and social media, I can't get the word out or provide a way for people to contact me. The events themselves require me to store and work with mounds of fancy things. None of that can come into an Amish home."

"True. But if you narrowed the types of parties to ones the bishop would approve and if you had a small shop built on a far corner of the land, a place with internet and computers and storage for all the fancy party stuff, what would you think of that?"

"It's a wonderful idea. I guess I was thinking all or nothing when it came to planning Englisch events."

"I think the bishop had that same mindset, but it's a funny thing about giving people time while you pray. Miracles happen, especially around Christmastime, when people focus on love and grace more than rules and religious expectations."

"So he's on board with a modified version of event planning?"

"He is. Specifics to be worked out between the two of you."

"Wow." She looked heavenward, seeing the North Star. She turned to Arlan. "Denki."

He lifted her gloved hand and rubbed it with his thumb. "The bishop and I talked about one other thing."

"Must've been quite the conversation."

"It has to do with me living at the farm." He looked her in the eyes. "Ivy, when we met, we were on opposite sides of the world. I was so mired in the rules of everything. You vexed and confused me."

"Well, probably because at the time I was too focused on breaking free of all the rules to see the value of our way of life."

"But somehow we've crossed all that distance and met in the middle. And I like you. A lot. Would" — he paused as if searching for words — "it be possible for us to court?"

After all their spirited discussions during the past six months, *now* he was nervous? It was adorable.

"Ya, Arlan. We can court. You took me on a Christmas buggy ride, and we're strolling downtown, so I think we're already courting." She laughed. "And I like you too."

"Gut." He cradled her face. "Very gut, ya?"

She nodded, unable to find her voice.

"With me living on the farm, we'll have to be careful. I won't enter the house with you inside unless your Mamm, Red, or Magda is there too."

"Which is basically all the time."

"Ya, but still. We'll have to make sure we live like neighbors — you in the big house and me in the carriage house."

"Wait, I think I liked being a girlfriend better than being a neighbor. Which is it, Arlan? Pick a lane." She elbowed him in the side.

He pulled her into a hug. "I pick the one that lets us travel down life's road together."

Christmas Eve, one year later
Dozens of candles lit the room, and a fire burned in the hearth as Ivy spread a large thick quilt over the living room floor. Cold winds howled. Arlan pulled the opposite side of the quilt across the clean floor to smooth it out, and then he sat down on the brick stoop in front of the fire, acting as a barrier if the baby should toddle that direction.

He was a good uncle. The best. And this past year of courting had showed her not only how good a man he was but how much fun they could have together as they walked through the challenges of life. They were a strong team, and she thanked God that Arlan had smashed his way into her life.

Arlan had purchased a herd of goats, and he and Red had put up new fences, dividing the cows from the goats. Goat milk sold really well, and the men were a solid team that made good profits, whether selling cow or goat milk. Magda and Mamm used the goat milk to make yogurt and cheese to sell locally.

Ivy now had a tiny shop built nowhere in sight of this house, and it had two computers, high-speed internet, and oodles of storage for all the fancy party things. Tegan worked by her side.

Her thoughts faded, and she turned her attention to the people in the room with her. The quilt Arlan and she were smoothing across the floor was for extra padding for the new walker. Magda's little Emanuel turned one just four days ago and had taken his first steps yesterday. The little guy squawked in his mother's lap and tried to get down.

Magda laughed and held him in place. "Hold your horses. Ivy's almost ready for you to get down."

"Kumm." From the recliner Red held out his arms, and Emanuel's eyes lit up. "Speaking of horses, we'll do the horsey game."

The baby boy wriggled free of his Mamm's arms and reached for Red. " 'Ed!"

Magda grinned and passed him over. Red started bouncing the little one on his knee.

Ivy looked at Arlan. He raised a brow and nodded before winking at her. They both thought something was going on between Magda and Red of late. A few months back Red had told Arlan that the baby kept him up too much and asked if Arlan would share the carriage house room. Arlan said yes, and the two men built a room divider in the long carriage house, and they started living as roommates, leaving the house to the women and baby. Maybe Red's reason for moving out of the house wasn't just about avoiding the baby crying at night. Maybe he had feelings for Magda and thought it best to move out of the house so that he and Magda weren't living under the same roof. The community would frown on them courting if they lived in the same house.

Ivy sat next to Arlan and laid her head on his shoulder. Arlan kissed her forehead. She loved this man more than she'd known was possible. How much would she love him in ten years? Or twenty? Or a lifetime?

"There you go, little man." Red set the toddler on his feet, but when he did, the boy seemed confused about where to go.

Holly came into the room with two hot chocolates in hand. "You're all sure you don't want some hot cocoa?"

The others shook their heads.

"Ivy." Holly passed a mug to her. "Did I tell you who came to see me at the pharmacy the other day?" She walked to the couch to sit next to Joshua.

"Denki." Ivy took a sip. "Who?"

"I saw your Swartzentruber friend, one of the girls who used to clean homes with you."

Ivy sat up straight. "Eva?"

"Ya. Because of HIPAA laws, you know I'm not allowed to tell you if she purchased anything, but I thought you might want to know that she and her Mamm came to Greene's."

Reading between the lines, she realized her sister was letting her know that Eva's Mamm had finally allowed her daughter to get treatment for her asthma. Thank goodness. After the local Swartzentruber community found out that the Zooks were housing Arlan and Magda last year, Dora and Eva's parents had closed all contact between the girls and Ivy. All Ivy could do was respect their wishes and pray they would seek treatment before it was too late.

"Thank you for telling me." Ivy held the warm cup close to her chest, savoring its sweet aroma.

Unlike the dark days after her Daed died, Ivy's heart often felt like a spring calf freed from its stall. A decade ago she'd been sure that life and Christmastime would never hold complete happiness again, not like it had when Daed was alive. They still missed him. Always would. But life was big enough to hold all the love and all the sadness and to keep moving forward.

What a lovely Christmas Eve. Ivy and the caroling group had sung at a frozen pond earlier in the day, and now Holly and Josh were visiting the Zook farm. They'd stay overnight and then go home after breakfast to be at the farm when all of Josh's siblings, their spouses, and their children arrived.

Josh and Holly hadn't said anything yet, but Ivy was sure her sister was expecting. Holly was barely showing, but it was easy to see on her slight frame. How many children would fill these farmhouse rooms in the Christmases to come? Her Daed would've loved it.

"Oh." Holly jumped up and reached into her dress pocket. "Lyle gave me this earlier today for you, Arlan." She took a few steps toward him and passed him an envelope.

Arlan opened it and peeked inside. It was a card. Ivy peered over his shoulder as he pulled it from the envelope. Inside were five one-hundred-dollar bills.

Arlan cleared his throat and began to read the handwritten words on the card: "Merry Christmas, Arlan and Ivy. Congratulations on your upcoming wedding! From Lyle and the rest of Greene's Pharmacy. Arlan, I have the last payment covered. Thanks for staying the course."

Ivy squeezed his arm. Giving this money was just like Lyle. During the past year Arlan had been diligently making payments for the damage to the storefront, sending Lyle five hundred dollars a month until the debt was paid off.

Arlan's brother had written, saying that he would pay back Arlan's investment a little at a time when he could and that he looked forward to seeing Arlan one day. It was a good start. Ivy doubted she and Arlan would be allowed into their home, but a visit at a nearby restaurant or maybe under shade trees in the yard would be very welcome.

Arlan had found it necessary to leave his people, but she hadn't needed to leave the Amish to find fulfillment. Life and love were a party anywhere a person chose to celebrate and honor them, and rules were a part of life.

ACKNOWLEDGMENTS

Adam Woodsmall, Erin's husband, thank you as always for sharing your knowledge about pharmacy and medicine, and thank you for entertaining and caring for our children with such enthusiasm and joy while we worked on this labor of love.

Debbie Pulley, Kay Johnson, and Missy Burgess, midwives with Atlanta Birth Care, thank you for your excellent care during the births of Silas and Lincoln and also for teaching me much about home birth — knowledge that was so valuable in writing this book.

Tommy Woodsmall, Cindy's husband, thank you for always being willing to share your farming and life experiences with us.

Shweta Woodsmall, Cindy's daughter-in-law, thank you for listening to the story ideas and answering the many questions about regulations and independent pharmacies.

Shannon Marchese, executive editor, thank you for always giving your best, for your support, sound advice, and attention to detail.

Carol Bartley, my line editor, thank you for your focus, humor, and diligence for all twenty-five works. If I can bribe you out of retirement for any part of my writing journey, I always will!

Laura Wright, senior production editor, thank you for making the transition from my former beloved production editor to my new one go so very smoothly! I look forward to editing more books with you.

Everyone at WaterBrook, an imprint of Penguin Random House, from marketing to sales to production to editorial, we've had fourteen years together and you are still the *best*!

Jaemor Farms and the Georgia Agricultural Commodity Commission, thank you for all you have to offer, from hands-on experience to a mobile dairy classroom — that allowed us time with a dairy cow — to answering many questions.

ABOUT THE AUTHORS

Cindy Woodsmall is the *New York Times* and CBA best-selling author of twenty-four works of fiction. She's best known for her Amish fiction. Her connection with the Amish community has been widely featured in national media outlets, including the *Wall Street Journal* and ABC *Nightline.* Cindy has won numerous awards and has been a finalist for the prestigious Christy, Rita, and Carol Awards. She lives outside Atlanta with her husband, just a short distance from her children and grandchildren.

Erin Woodsmall is a writer, musician, wife, and mom. She has edited, brainstormed, and researched books with her mother-in-law, Cindy Woodsmall, for the last decade. The two also coauthored *The Gift of Christmas Past, As the Tide Comes In,* and *The Christmas Remedy.*

The employees of Thorndike Press hope you have enjoyed this Large Print book. All our Thorndike, Wheeler, and Kennebec Large Print titles are designed for easy reading, and all our books are made to last. Other Thorndike Press Large Print books are available at your library, through selected bookstores, or directly from us.

For information about titles, please call:
　(800) 223-1244

or visit our website at:
　gale.com/thorndike

To share your comments, please write:
　Publisher
　Thorndike Press
　10 Water St., Suite 310
　Waterville, ME 04901